A Candlelight Ecstasy Romance ™

THERE WAS SOMETHING
SO INTENSELY EXCITING,
SO FORBIDDEN, SO SWEET . . .

The lightning flashed again and again, accompanied by the harsh crack of thunder as Ann urged Nathan on. The hayloft formed a natural nest. They were in a cocoon, safe from the elements. His lips were soft and generous. She could feel desire radiating through his great frame. Nathan's eyes were closed as he moved in subtle urgency to take her for his own.

She realized as she came to her senses that she barely knew this man. She had let this go much too far. In shock she pushed him from her, using all the strength she could muster.

"No!" she cried, shaking her head. "No!"

SPEAK SOFTLY TO MY SOUL

Dorothy Ann Bernard

A CANDLELIGHT ECSTASY ROMANCE™

Published by
Dell Publishing Co., Inc.
1 Dag Hammarskjold Plaza
New York, New York 10017

Dell ® TM 681510, Dell Publishing Co., Inc.

Candlelight Ecstasy Romance™ is a trademark of
Dell Publishing Co., Inc., New York, New York.

ISBN 0–440–18827–X

Printed in the United States of America
First printing—December 1982

To my mother,
Daisy Belle Haegele

To Our Readers:

We have been delighted with your enthusiastic response to Candlelight Ecstasy Romances™, and we thank you for the interest you have shown in this exciting series.

In the upcoming months we will continue to present the distinctive sensuous love stories you have come to expect only from Ecstasy. We look forward to bringing you many more books from your favorite authors and also the very finest work from new authors of contemporary romantic fiction.

As always, we are striving to present the unique, absorbing love stories that you enjoy most—books that are more than ordinary romance.

Your suggestions and comments are always welcome. Please write to us at the address below.

Sincerely,

The Editors
Candlelight Romances
1 Dag Hammarskjold Plaza
New York, New York 10017

CHAPTER ONE

The afternoon was bleak and Ann Taylor stood with her back against the wind, shivering in the middle of an old farmyard. The roof of the house was caved in on one side and dark, dirty windowpanes gave it an eerie, haunted air. Weather-beaten boards and peeling paint protected its useless skeleton. She brought her hand to her brow and glanced out across the weed-strewn, rutted yard where a once-red barn stood in a condition of semicollapse. Wisps of aged and rotted hay hung from its sagging loft, clinging to misshapen, weather-warped boards. An old windmill creaked and a chill wind stirred an old porch swing. Mist was settling on fragments of fences in weed-clogged rows. She followed their trek as they rolled gently outward over the fields, toward the muddy clearing of a newly emerging housing project.

She felt chilled and depressed as the wind whipped about, encircling her throat until it grew unbearably tight, finally forcing a warm tear from beneath her eyelids. She kicked the muddy turf, sighed, and wiped her eyes with the back of her hand. She should never have come here. This had been one of Jeff's favorite spots. More than once he had scared her witless with his haunted house and ghost stories when they played here. The house had always been deserted as long as she could remember.

"Oh, well," she sighed. "You're here now, so get on with it. . . ."

She trudged back to her car and drove slowly over the rutted path to a tiny two-lane road. Although there was a nip in the air the gloom was challenged by the emerging green of early spring.

Ann thought back over her early childhood in this small farm community nestled in central Ohio. In retrospect it seemed to be an existence of grueling hard work, devoid of poetry except for a few bright notes here and there, as the seasons churned out their predictable delights.

She smiled as she recalled shyly reciting the first poem she had ever written to Jeff and remembered as he pantomimed it back to her in great dramatic sweeps.

"The world is like a cake," she had said, as he spread his hands in wide circles and created swirling frosting.

"Green spring has all things mixed,
Summer comes to bake,"

He mixed furiously, giving a fair imitation of a frantic eggbeater.

"Autumn comes to cool,"

He blew in exaggerated theatrics as she went on, giggling now.

"And Winter comes to frost . . ."

But before she could finish he effected a hysterical swooping finale and they both collapsed in laughter. Then she remembered the stern "ahem" as her father walked into the cow barn and they scurried to get on with the milking. They were always protective of each other, as only twins, in some special telepathic way, can be.

As memories continued to pour over her she turned out

onto State Highway 310 and headed for the small town of Pataskala. She drove over the smooth rolling asphalt and girded herself for the coming ordeal. She was about to do something she had sworn she would never do.

She rounded a curve at the edge of town and reversed her direction. Purposely she began to slow down as she came to the entrance of the Pataskala Cemetery and slowly began to wind her way through narrow gravel drives and a field of pretentious tombstones. She stopped the car when she came to the big monolithic stone designating the Taylor family. Behind it and all around there were stones of various sizes dating back more than a hundred years. She walked until she found it and then she stood, hollow and spent, unable to weep as she read noncommittally, "Jeffrey Wayne Taylor." She refused to acknowledge the years and the youth proclaimed by the dates.

A longing swept over her as she remembered her twin, how close they had been until that fateful day when they had broken apart. He, to enlist in the service and ship out to Vietnam, and she, to man the pickets in the long lines of war protesters, so noisy and strident in the late sixties and early seventies. Now he lay here, sent home draped in a flag, while she had struggled on, angry and unhappy, lonely for him, far away from their roots and swearing vehemently that she would never do what she was doing this very moment.

She had fled, refusing to attend the funeral, making no effort to find a peace that could temper her grief, driven, until now at last at the age of thirty-one she had decided to come home and say good-bye to him. She reached out to touch the smooth stone, allowing her fingers to trail over it. Memory after memory washed over her, somehow cleansing rather than depressing her as she felt the warmth of a love, unlike any other she had ever known, settle once again in her heart. A tear threatened, but didn't emerge as she touched her fingers to her lips and pressed them to the cold stone with a little smile.

She arose, not remembering when she had actually kneeled, and met the intense gaze of a man vaguely familiar to her who stood several family plots away. She hadn't noticed anyone else being there when she first arrived, but now she saw the dusty pickup truck, nearly hidden by a winding curve.

She could barely make out the large letters forming the name Warner on the family stone near where he stood. Nathan Warner. She remembered him now. He had been several years ahead of her in high school, already married and a father before she graduated.

Blue eyes met blue eyes and locked as Ann's short curly hair blew about, accenting the brightness of her eyes and the color in her cheeks. She pursed her lips and continued to stare at him as the wind whipped the long scarf over her stylish spring coat, brushing it against the high tops of her fashionable kid boots.

She reached unconsciously to calm the flyaway chestnut locks of her hair and noted his rugged appearance. He was a big man, yet even from this distance he emanated a gentleness and humbleness as he looked away, glancing first at the ground, and then the sky. He nervously fingered the tractor cap in his hand. Yet, there was an undeniable strength, too. She saw his jaw clench when he pulled his hat down snugly over unruly hair, shadowing strong chiseled features. He turned resolutely away, avoiding any communication they might have had when he stepped into the truck and drove away.

Ann stood silently for a few moments longer and then, after a final second with Jeff, made her departure. As she drove by the Warner plots she noted one perfect, pink rose on a slightly elevated grassy rectangle. She also saw a date on the headstone that indicated this day as an anniversary.

When she clattered out onto the road from the graveled drive, she headed thoughtfully into Pataskala, a beautiful sleepy little town which she had avoided for more than a dozen years. As she drove over the bridge of the South Fork Creek and headed down Main Street, she observed that little had changed, including the stately trees and old, well-kept houses that lined the way.

She came to the center of town, passing the buff, square Pataskala Banking Company. After her years in Chicago it looked diminished and disappointingly small. *How the years go by,* she thought to herself as the bank clock struck the hour.

She smiled in fond memory as she crossed the railroad tracks and drove on out to Highway 16. Here at last the progress of the intervening years was evident, as she had to consciously search for the turn onto the county road which she had once traveled almost unconsciously. Soon she was again on familiar territory, not far from her first stop at the old Harding farm. She finally came to the Taylor homestead which proclaimed its heritage on a big sign over the entrance to a neat gravel drive. It led back to a tree-lined yard surrounding the house on a farm that had been home to eight generations of Taylors.

"Mom," she called as she stepped out of her car. "I'm here."

Hastily she glanced around at all of the familiar buildings, as her small, portly mother came rushing from the square two-story house painted in a traditional antique yellow.

"Well, I see you've finally gotten here," she cried, as she enfolded her willowy daughter in a warm hug. "I've been waiting for you all day and Mr. Shuman has called from the county extension office wondering what time you would arrive."

Ann smiled in response to her mother's fluttery welcome, well aware of the deceptive facade that hid a will of iron not easily reckoned with if you happened to be the recipient of her displeasure.

"I see you're alone," she said, very straightforward, not bothering to hide the unspoken implication of her words.

"Yes, Mom, I'm alone. Jim and I are no longer together."

"Well, I should say it's about time. I don't know," she said with self-righteous emphasis, "what's gotten into you young folks today—living together and not getting married. Here you are, good-looking and college educated and just throwing it all away—"

"I know, I know, Mom," said Ann, breaking in hastily, and well she did know as old antagonisms and conflicts from the past threatened to rear their ugly heads, but she smiled, her emotions tempered now by a hard-won maturity.

Though her parents were proud of her success, the career she'd carved out for her herself in the competitive field of public relations and the executive position she had held at Green Valley Farms, Ann knew only too well they had never approved of the more rebellious side of her nature.

The final blow had come when she had elected to live with Jim Stanton, an insurance executive, in a relationship

14

that lasted four years, rather than adhering to the traditional ties of matrimony. She realized it must have been a real burden to her parents, and yet, while they voiced their disapproval, they never once withdrew their love. For a moment Ann felt a genuine pang of regret, sorry now that she had hurt them.

She realized in that instant that this house, the house she had grown up in, was a place to visit and remember in. It was not the place where she should live. She had managed to save a sizable nest egg in her well-paid position with Green Valley Farms and had then prudently invested it during the past few years. Now she had a much more conservative and moderately paying position as a county extension agent. But she was sure that, having the ability to make a hefty down payment, she would be able to find something she could afford, allowing her the security of close family ties and the luxury of her independence.

She grabbed one or two of her bags and began to follow her bustling mother. As she walked through the door of the house she had not set foot in in years, it suddenly seemed diminished from her memory of it. It had always seemed to be an enormous, roomy house, spacious security enveloping the memories of her childhood, which she had admittedly embellished as the years had gone by. The high-ceilinged large kitchen of her memory, while still cozy and folksy, seemed little more than an ordinary-size room now. The rest of the house also seemed to close in on her as she followed the familiar steps to her room, still furnished in bright and cheerful organdy. Little had changed since her departure to college, years before.

Seeking some diversion from these unexpected homecoming impressions, Ann began to chitchat unconsciously with her mother about her activities before arriving.

"I stopped over at the old Harding farm on the way in. . . . You know, we used to play over there all of . . ."

Ann stopped when she realized her mother was astutely appraising her.

"I . . . I . . . noticed it was for sale," she went on hastily, as she realized she had inadvertently, perhaps subconsciously, plunged into a dangerous emotional area. "You'd think those people from the housing development would grab that up."

She looked away as her mother continued to peruse her in perceptive silence.

"I expect," Mrs. Taylor finally answered, "those developer people have got all they can do to sell what they've got, now that the market is so bad. As I recall, though, that was one of your brother Jeff's favorite places. Have you come home, daughter, to make your peace?"

Blunt and to the point as always, her steel-blue eyes squarely met those of her daughter, but Ann also sensed a real softening, something extraspecial she hadn't experienced from her mother since she had been a very little girl.

Feeling bolstered, she took a deep breath and decided to plunge on.

"Yes, Mom, I guess maybe I have. I went on over to the cemetery and I think . . . Oh, I don't know," she said, feeling suddenly foolish. "Anyway," she continued after a big breath, "I'm glad I did. . . . But you'll never guess," she said in a rush, "who I saw there."

"Well, no, I guess I couldn't imagine," said Mrs. Taylor. "Just about anyone from around here could have a reason to be there, I guess."

"Nathan Warner," said Ann. "You know he was a few years ahead of me, used to show cattle at the fairs with us.

16

He looked so dejected and . . . I don't know. I guess he didn't recognize me—didn't speak or wave or anything."

"Nate Warner, sure I know him. Funny thing about him. You know he married the Tate girl, they were so young and everything, had a baby right away, too, but those two sure put it together. Both of them worked their way through college and had one of the best farm operations anyone has ever seen around here. They were sure stuck on each other and then seven or eight years ago she suddenly got sick and died within a year. He's never been quite the same. . . ."

She paused as she wiped her hands on her apron, musing in obvious pity for him. Ann did nothing to discourage her mother's discussion. She was honestly glad for this diversion from her own emotions, as the vision of the lone rose on the grassy knoll once again manifested itself.

"You know," her mother went on, "he was always such a happy-go-lucky fellow, always cheerful and optimistic. He still is to some degree, but there's always this touch of melancholy about him. He's got those two teen-age kids, but he's never been serious about another woman in all these years and Lord knows, as good-looking as he is, plenty have tried. . . . Then too," she went on, "he's gone almost a little crazy, changing his whole farm setup to a natural, organic one, but I've got to hand it to him. He seems to be just as successful as he ever was."

Ann looked at her mother, somewhat puzzled.

"Do you mean he doesn't use any modern equipment or farming methods? He's farming like Grandpa did or something?"

"No, not exactly. But I expect you'll hear a whole lot more about it when you get to work next week. He's constantly got the agriculture extension office in an uproar."

"Well," said Ann, as she came and gave her mother a hug, "I think I'm going to have to do a lot of catching up."

Her mother was momentarily flustered by Ann's unexpected gesture of affection, but she was obviously pleased as she bustled to answer the insistent ring of the telephone in the kitchen below.

A moment later she called to Ann that Mr. Shuman was on the telephone. "And everyone else will know it, too," she said as she handed the receiver to Ann. "I can hear the party line a-clicking all the way to Newark!"

Ann laughed as she greeted her new boss.

"Hello, Mr. Shuman. How nice to hear from you. . . ."

But as she talked to him, mouthing practiced, gracious phrases, unconsciously the image of Nathan Warner standing so alone and vulnerable played in the back of her mind. In a way she almost felt as if they had spoken. Realizing her thoughts were becoming just a bit melodramatic, not to mention inappropriate, she forced herself back to the conversation at hand.

Mr. Shuman had been telling her about an upcoming round and square dance, a benefit sponsored by the 4-H. He thought it would be a good place for her to begin reacquainting herself with the community, and Ann wholeheartedly agreed.

"Yes, of course, Mr. Shuman, I'm looking forward to my work with you. I'll be in early Monday morning and the introduction at the dance sounds marvelous. I'm overwhelmed that you would go to so much trouble."

"Oh, and I hope you don't mind," said Mr. Shuman in his final remarks, "I've taken the liberty of asking Nathan

18

Warner to pick you up. He lives close by and I thought it might be a good idea if he were on good terms with at least one person in our office for a change. You know him, I'm sure. He says he remembers you as a little girl."

"Oh well, of course," said Ann. She could feel herself beginning to blush over this coincidence and her own private thoughts. "Mother was just mentioning his rather unconventional methods."

"Unconventional, all right." Ann could almost picture him grimacing. "But he's nevertheless a smart man and a good farmer. He's not all wrong and we'd sure like to be on better terms with him here in our office. Guess you won't mind if we take advantage of you right away," he said with a little chuckle, as if in response to his own private little joke. "It's not every day that we have such an experienced public relations person to call upon."

When Ann hung up the phone for the first time she felt a little odd about some of her past decisions concerning her life-style. Never before had she felt any semblance of guilt or wrongdoing, but somehow she sensed a feeling of sly, knowing innuendo about Mr. Shuman's last remark and it made her feel distinctly uncomfortable. Obviously in a community so small and conservative, where people tended to know everyone, she had expected a few raised eyebrows. But now she felt an almost insidious premonition that she had perhaps underestimated that response in comparison to the cold indifference that characterized her recent urban life.

She paused as she sank down into one of her mother's many comfortable rockers and noted the attractive framing of some of her grandmother's crocheted doilies, which her mother had metamorphosed into modern stylish accents. Ann listened to her mother bustle around the kitchen. She knit her brow in unconscious concentration as she began to analyze the past few years of her life.

After college she had fortunately landed an entry-level job in the publicity and promotions department of Green Valley Farms. Then, gifted with verve and creative flair, Ann soon achieved a high-paying and coveted public relations position there. She had traveled extensively and worked with the media in promoting products through new homemaking techniques and recipes tested in the giant laboratory kitchens in the home offices in Chicago. It was glamorous and exciting, but very high pressured. She had begun to feel vaguely dissatisfied and finally faced up to the fact that her work was simply not giving her the kind of personal fulfillment she needed. Perhaps she was expecting too much. But Ann knew that at this stage of her life her values had perhaps changed. Monetary rewards, glamour, and a prestigious position were simply not enough anymore.

She sighed as she reached for a popular women's magazine and began to leaf through it. She couldn't help but notice all of the ads hawking products for stress and fatigue accompanied by dozens of products to keep you young and thin. They were an insidious threat attempting to make her paranoid about her advancing maturity. When, in reality, she felt good about her age, as if she had just begun to live after surviving all of her youthful conflicts.

She flipped the page and a tanned, smiling man in smart, casual tennis attire came into view. She was immediately reminded of Jim and her four-year excursion into the so-called land of freedom. It had seemed such a smart, chic thing to do. She wasn't ready for a commitment and with all of her travel it seemed that she could have her cake and eat it, too. It was so simple. She and Jim were adults and they understood each other perfectly, but in the end it was that very lack of commitment that had caused the relationship to fall apart, ending ultimately in a state of detachment and total dispassion.

She wondered if it would have been any different had there been vows to consider and the accompanying guilt of breaking them. In the end there had been nothing, absolutely nothing. After the heat and pathos of the initial conflicts they had just gradually allowed it to wear down, more out of convenience than anything else. As she looked at the picture she had little or no emotion other than an older but wiser pang of regret, wishing it could have been more. . . .

Then there was this gnawing from deep inside, which had finally managed to surface. It left her uneasy as she began to come to terms with her past. Memories of her childhood and Jeff in particular became an obsession until finally she had realized that she was deeply ashamed of her cowardice when she ran away.

She got up, throwing the magazine aside, and clutched herself as she walked restlessly around the room. She knew she couldn't change the past and she certainly couldn't bring Jeff back, but something told her coming to terms with it was important. Strangely, now she had an unquenchable yearning for the caring and clucking concern which she once thought she hated. Ultimately, she wasn't satisfied and she was just plain lonely.

So, in one decisive moment, she had decided to go home. It had seemed fateful when she made an initial inquiry and learned that a county extension agent position was available so close by.

"Did I hear you say over the phone that Nathan Warner is taking you to the dance?" Mrs. Taylor had come in, wiping flour from her hands after putting several cherry pies into the oven. "Isn't that kind of strange? You know, your paw and I are planning to go, too."

Ann smiled. She realized how good it felt to hear these questions, as she also remembered how angry they would once have made her.

"Well, to tell you the truth, Mom, I don't know. But I guess if I'm going to work for this man I need to stay on his good side. He arranged this and asked me to go along with it and I can't really see any harm in it so long as Nathan doesn't mind, either. It sure is a coincidence though, isn't it?"

"Well, maybe, maybe not," she answered. "You never know about these things, do you?" she ended sagely.

Ann smiled and gave her mother another affectionate pat as she arose and stretched languidly. "I guess not," she said teasingly, "but right now I think I'll go and get into some jeans and go out and find Dad."

"That sounds like a good idea. He's out around the barn someplace. He's been looking for you all day, but you know how he is. He don't want to seem too anxious."

She went up the stairs two at a time almost as if she were an ungainly adolescent again and quickly donned designer jeans and blouse covered by a bright colorful windbreaker. She went bounding down the stairs again and bounced out through her mother's spacious screened porch, which must have boasted more than a half dozen rocking chairs in various sizes and modes. They sat about in a hodge-podge of plants accented by bright pillows and other folksy country touches which created an ambience of welcome and contentment. The sunlight streaming in and the delicious aroma of the baking cherry pies made Ann think of knitting and other homey things.

As she stepped out onto the wet lawn the invigorating tang of the air teased with just a touch of balminess. Lilacs were just beginning to emerge. The maple leaves were still tiny and sparse; the sun, filtering through the tree branches, outlined them brightly. She could feel burdens which she had forced herself not to examine too closely lifting from her. She smiled and knew the yard would soon be a marvelous riot of spring flower colors.

She stuck her hands deeply into her windbreaker and headed on towards the familiar barn where once she had helped with the feeding of baby calves and the seemingly unending dairy farm chores. She saw her father on a tractor coming across the field. He saw her and began to wave. Soon he came noisily through a heavy wooden gate, which she struggled to open for him.

As he scrambled eagerly down from the high seat he greeted her a little self-consciously. "Just like old times," he said heartily. "You know we can always use a good hand around here."

Ann went to him and embraced him warmly. She was suddenly speechless, as the emotion of seeing him just as he had always been threatened to overcome her.

"Good to see you, daughter," he said huskily through her whipping hair. "How have you been?"

"Fine, Dad, fine," she said, as she laughingly gained control of her emotions, belied only by vestiges of telltale brightness in her eyes. "It feels wonderful to be back home again."

"Well, it's wonderful having you. Your maw and I are getting on and we really miss not having a young'n around once in a while."

He was a big man and his eyes were filled with a gentle humor, but his demeanor portrayed the solemn contemplative man who embodied his inner existence.

Ann looked out across what used to be the cow yard. It was peculiarly empty now. "Looks like you've made some changes around here," she said, gesturing toward the barn.

"Yeah," he sighed. "Even with the new-fangled milking parlor I just couldn't keep up with the dairy anymore and the return on the investment necessary to keep up just didn't seem worth it to me, so I'm just sticking to corn and other grains now. I miss the cows, though. I always liked the rhythm of the dairy, but I guess there's nothing wrong with having a little time for reflection in your old age, either."

"Oh, Dad, you're not old," she said teasingly.

But she reflected inwardly on the new and unfamiliar vocabulary of her father, who sounded more like a Wall Street broker than a simple man who made his living from the land. It dawned on her then that there was truth in the rhetoric she had been hearing unconsciously over the past years indicating that farming was no longer a way of life, but in reality just another cold, dispassionate business. She thought of all the technologies and advances in modern farming, of all the businesses that had sprung up around them, and realized that the pastoral existence of her childhood was gone forever. Somehow, that left her with a feeling of real sadness.

Yet, here she was surrounded by the sounds and sights of emerging spring all jumbled and exciting, just as she had always remembered it, and she knew the spirit of that existence was still very much alive. It was simply a question of intelligent discernment and wise country savvy

24

which had always held the big city at bay. It was still alive in men like her father and Nathan Warner.

She was startled as the name of this man once again intruded into her thoughts. Part of her new job would involve a talent for educating and guiding the farm community toward modern developments. She had no reason to align herself at this stage with this man, a man she barely remembered and certainly knew nothing about. She realized perceptively that she had somehow made some sort of mental tie with him during those few moments in the cemetery and now she was going to have to be very careful lest she lose her objectivity before she had even begun her work.

Almost as if to illustrate the old saying, "speak of the devil," a pickup truck turned into the lane. Ann recognized it immediately as the one she had seen in the cemetery. The truck crunched and popped its way into the gravel farmyard and Nathan Warner swung himself out of the truck in one practiced motion. She hadn't remembered him being so tall.

"Afternoon, Jake," he said, the embodiment of jocularity. "Thought I'd stop by and see if Shuman from the county extension office had ever reached Ann and to see if she was in . . ."

He had gradually become aware of Ann's presence and consciously recognized her from their earlier, fleeting meeting as his speech slowed to a hesitant drawl.

"By golly," he said, looking at her with an impish smile. "I almost didn't recognize you. Goin' away to the big city and dressing up so smart. It takes a pair of jeans to jog the old memory," he said a tad sheepishly.

As he addressed his remarks to Ann after shaking her father's hand and clapping him on the shoulder she perceptively realized this was his unspoken way of apologizing for his lack of greeting at the cemetery. She also understood that he didn't wish to make reference to that meeting. She could almost sense the pain it would cause him, just as she also realized this was not the emotionally naked, vulnerable man she had seen there. This was a smooth, confident man hiding behind a facade of folksy good nature.

His eyes met hers. His tanned, rugged features were a picture of friendliness. He extended his hand and greeted her cordially. "Nice to see you again," he said softly, almost reflectively, as his eyes roamed freely over her face. He seemed to approve of the abandon of her blowing curls as they whipped around her wide doe eyes and got caught up in the moistness of her ruby lips. "Looks like, if it's all right with you," he continued as he finally released her hand, "we've got a date for Saturday night. Thought I'd stop by and see if it suited you or not."

As he talked Ann had the silliest nostalgic sensation. She could hear slow melodious waltz music and smell roses as she pictured a couple dancing romantically over a green lawn, totally incongruous with the homey nature of his address. But at the thought of roses the vision shattered painfully as she visualized again the lonely pink rose left earlier in a sad, sad place.

She shook her head and forced herself to respond. Again she noted his rough clothes and seeming nonchalance. She was having a few second thoughts. "Well, it was awfully thoughtful of Mr. Shuman to take the trouble to make arrangements with you. And certainly kind of you to agree," she said sincerely, "but Mom and Dad are planning to go, too. I hate to put you to extra trouble."

"No trouble, not at all," he said. "As a matter of fact,

26

my kids, Christopher and Tanya are going, too. No reason why we can't all go in my station wagon. It's more than forty miles to the fairgrounds where the dance is being held."

"Sounds like a good idea to me," said Ann's father. "It'll save gas, and save me some driving, too." He ended with a droll little chuckle.

"Well, I'm glad you agree," said Nathan as he gave a sly wink in Ann's direction.

The aroma of the baking pies was now beginning to permeate the entire farmyard. Nathan began to sniff appreciatively as he touched Ann's arm and gestured toward the house. "Think I'll go up and say hello to Mrs. Taylor," he said with a big grin on his face. "Better make sure our plans are all right with her, too."

As he talked he had begun unconsciously to guide Ann along with him, moving toward the house. She couldn't help but be amazed at this rather forward man who was obviously not at all the way she had pictured him after that first touching scene in the cemetery.

"Well," he said teasingly, with a touch of intimacy and obvious appreciation in his voice as they crunched along, "looks like Shuman is putting you to work right away— pulling out all the stops, sending the ladies after me now . . ."

Ann looked at him in genuine surprise as her father trudged slowly behind them safely out of earshot.

Nathan grinned, obviously enjoying himself. "I'm looking forward to a real good time." He raised his eyebrows in laughing exaggerated theatrics. "From what I hear, a city girl like yourself should know how to have a good time."

Ann was appalled, but before she could voice her in-

27

stant displeasure they were opening the door and her mother was bustling to meet them. Within moments they were once again caught up in a jocular, neighborly conversation. His teasing tone of seconds before was no longer evident as Nathan greeted Ann's mother warmly and showered her with appreciative comments about the emerging cherry pies.

Why, he's almost as witty and urbane as the most practiced cad I've ever met, thought Ann to herself as she watched him in authentic amazement. Her concept of Nathan Warner was rapidly changing with the passing of every second on her mother's huge kitchen clock.

CHAPTER TWO

She didn't know why she was doing this. The soft swish of the windshield wipers gave a whispering emphasis to her thoughts as the teasing mist threatened to become another early spring downpour. She drove by the Harding farm again, noting the name of the realtor, and then drove carefully on. Almost as if compelled by some outer force she finally came to the neat drive of the Warner farm. She paused, took a deep breath, and willed her shaking hands to cease their idiocy.

She was acting on an impulse much against her better judgment. Nathan had gone on to jokingly commandeer one of her mother's cherry pies during that initial visit and then in passing before he left mentioned that Ann might want to stop in and take a look at his operation. "Before," as he put it, "Shuman has a chance to totally indoctrinate you and ruin your perspective."

She had been amazed by his sudden use of polished, intellectual vocabulary and realized his use of a folksy facade belied the existence of a learned inner man. She was frankly fascinated and had been unable to shake him from her thoughts. Finally, in disgust, feeling much like a giggling adolescent, she had decided to go out for a drive and before she knew it she was about to turn into his lane.

Realizing how foolish her actions were, she was just about to turn around and head back home when suddenly the roar of a powerful tractor startled her. She jumped and killed the engine of her car when the brake and clutch warred with one another.

She looked up and saw Nathan's grinning eyes, his pleasure at the sight of her evident, even through the pouring rain. He motioned from the tractor cab for her to follow. She was committed now and to turn away would be even more foolish than the initial impulse to come here in the first place.

"Well, you made your bed, now you'll have to lie in it," she said out loud as she mouthed one of her mother's favorite sayings. "You wouldn't want to blow your image as a sophisticated city girl anyway," she ended flippantly, feeling much less confidence than her bravado indicated.

She restarted the car and followed the massive machine. Its gigantic tires reminded her of miniature Ferris wheels as they churned through the gravel drive, spewing water and mud from their edges. From her recollections it had to be at least twice as big as any tractor she had ever seen or driven in her earlier years on the farm. As she pulled into the neat farmyard there was an air of organized industriousness.

Seconds later Nathan bounced down from the high cab and was futilely trying to dodge the rain as he came running to her car door and motioned her to drive into one of the big barns. As she drove quickly through the wide doors she was enveloped in the sweet clean smells of good hay and straw. It plunged her into an almost unbearable well of memory as she recalled the years of working in a barn such as this with Jeff never far from her side.

"Glad to see you could stop by," said Nathan, making

great sweeping motions to shake the water from his denim jacket. He pushed his hat to a roguish tilt, gallantly opened her car door and moved to assist her from the car. His hands were strong and sure as he grasped her arm in a familiar gesture. Ann felt as though his fingers were radiating heat gently all the way to her bone and her entire body responded warmly to his touch.

"I was out for a drive, planning to take a look at the Harding farm when I got caught in this downpour," she hedged artfully, hoping she could make this visit seem somewhat coincidental.

"Well, I'm mighty glad to have you," he said with a big grin. "Give me just a second and I'll show you around."

Ann glanced around the barn. It was not one of those cold, sterile corrugated buildings so prevalent on modern farms for all of the right cost-effective reasons. No, Nathan's family was also among the first homesteaders in the area and this was a huge, multipurpose barn, beautifully kept and preserved from another era, more than a hundred years old.

The rain came down softly, pattering on the shingled roof with a special warm hushed quality. It transported her unconsciously back more than twenty years. She was surrounded by the security of clean yellow straw used for warm bedding and the pungent smells of hay whispering through the slatted racks as the loafing animals grasped it and chewed in warm, murmuring contentment. She gravitated toward a pen of very young calves. She looked up toward the cavernous roof and instinctively checked to be sure all of the creatures were comfortable and well tended. She heard a rustling sound as Nathan returned and found her gazing dreamily about.

"This is a wonderful barn," she said. "I'd almost forgotten how marvelous these old barns are. It's as though the rest of the world doesn't exist and everything is under control here."

Nathan looked at her piercingly. For the first time since that first wordless encounter, Ann felt as if she were meeting the real Nathan Warner, stripped of all his churlish simplicity.

"Yes, this is a wonderful structure," he said. "It was built, believe it or not, with a pike and derrick at a barn-raising nearly a hundred and fifty years ago. The man who designed it must have been a natural architect."

He went on to point out various features, including marvelous carved openings for ventilation. Ann watched as his hands ran over heavy cast-iron hinges, enjoying very much this glimpse of the introspective, intelligent man Nathan kept so well hidden.

"Why," he said with a trace of his earlier jocularity, "this barn is so fancy that it even has stairs!"

Ann could feel herself being carried along with a heady buoyancy as Nathan's enthusiasm enveloped her. She looked out through the rain which was softening to a light patter, about to stop. She noted that the entire farmyard was organized in a way that preserved the integrity of a much earlier farm operation. Across the way there was a magnificent old house, much like the one she had grown up in.

It was a wonderful setting, almost like a recreated historical village. Nathan was just about to show her more when the quiet was shattered by the strident ring of a telephone, obviously located somewhere in the barn.

"Be with you in a minute," he said, moving hurriedly toward the sound. "About this time of year everything begins to move in high gear."

As he disappeared into the depths of the barn, Ann stepped outside and began to wander aimlessly around. The rain had almost stopped; the moisture-laden air felt good against her skin. Everything looked shiny and new. She walked toward the tractor she had followed moments earlier. She ran her hands over its smooth hood. On an impulse she grabbed the seat and began to hoist herself up. She remembered days of bone-tiring, hot work on tractors that didn't have cabs and recalled the way she and Jeff had worked together. For the first time she felt a sense of genuine warmth and gratitude for the simple fact that she had experienced the moments and he had shared them with her.

She maneuvered herself awkwardly into the big, cumbersome seat and became immediately aware of Nathan's long legs as she reached futilely for the clutch and brake pedals. She placed her hands on the steering wheel and began to peer at the mind-boggling array of dials.

"My God," she said out loud. "There's even a computer on this thing!"

As she bent more closely to examine the other gadgets and levers she lost her balance for just a second. Her hand flew out and she accidentally pressed one of the buttons. To her horror the great machine roared to life. The noise was devastating. Before she could release her petrified senses, Nathan came running from the barn.

"My God, woman!" he yelled. "What in the hell do you think you're doing?"

"I . . . I don't know. . . ."

"Get down from there," he ordered.

She looked at him in shock as the harshness of his words rebounded about her. The tractor shuddered and Nathan's hand shot out and switched the motor off. It sputtered and died in aggrieved rebellion and Ann felt herself begin to sag. She struggled to find her footing as she stepped from the tractor hitch to the ground.

"Be careful," said Nathan, his voice softening and his strong arms going out to steady her. "Here, let me help you." His eyes met hers a little sheepishly. "I'm sorry. I shouldn't have yelled at you like that."

She was relieved to hear some concern in his voice. She looked up at him and hated her feelings of weakness as she walked unsteadily on. Large drops of rain began to fall again, striking their faces with big splats. Nathan pulled her close and they ran toward the barn. The wind picked up suddenly and the huge barn doors banged back and forth. Straw, dirt, and branches began to swirl and one of the doors smashed toward Ann. She moved swiftly to avoid it and stumbled awkwardly. She bumped her head and felt herself falling. She never heard Nathan as he shouted, "Watch out!"

From a haze, surrounded by the pungent smells of sweet hay, she heard a soft voice pleading with her to be all right.

She moaned in response.

There was an urgency in his voice as Nathan's great frame bent over her, a note of genuine tenderness which was very comforting. It was like a dream, a wonderful dream. She was safe and warm, surrounded by a wonderful plethora of familiar aromas that somehow negated the fuzzy pain in her head. She was being held by someone who cared. She felt herself being lifted to a sitting position and her eyes fluttered open in obvious confusion.

She met the ashen bewildered gaze of Nathan and felt herself completely engulfed in naked emotion as he gathered her close to him.

"Come on, wake up," he urged as he gave her a gentle shake.

Ann felt herself responding with a natural warmth and tenderness. She buried her face in his chest and brought her arms up around his massive shoulders. "I'm sorry," she finally mumbled. "I was just sort of remembering when I was younger and used to drive the tractors. I only meant to sit in the seat . . ."

"Don't worry about it," he said. "It was an accident. You didn't hurt yourself when you fell?"

"No . . . No. I'm all right—just a little stunned."

He brought her chin up and his eyes met hers. "You're sure?" he said with emphasis. He reached out and tenderly touched her forehead which sported a small bruise.

She nodded.

A little smile began to creep around his eyes.

"Well, I'm sure glad you're okay, but I'll tell you one thing. . . . You've managed to scare the living hell out of me. Not once, but *twice* in less than five minutes."

She returned his smile and their eyes locked as the comforting sounds of the barnyard went on around them. Rain began to patter on the roof again and suddenly there was a great crack of lightning and thunder at the same time. Ann jumped as Nathan instinctively pulled her to him. They clutched each other as their lips came together in unison with the last rumbles of the breaking sky.

Slowly his lips caressed her in a tender exploration and she responded dreamily, feeling that the wonderful dream had returned as she pulled him closer, trailing her fingers over his ears and tousling his hair. His lips began a trail down her neck and for eons of seconds they were content to touch and caress tenderly in a slow and deliberate feast

35

of sensation until at last their fervor grew naturally stronger.

Ann knew she should be stopping this but she was momentarily spurred on by the natural, but provocative, feeling of their surroundings. There was something intensely exciting about kissing in the hay, the gentle sound of the rain on the roof, something free-spirited and forbidden. She wanted to savor the sweetness of such a pleasure. The lightning flashed again and again, accompanied by the harsh cracks of thunder, but they were in a cocoon, safe from the elements, surrounded by the snugness of a natural nest. She settled into Nathan's protective embrace.

With a deep moan she pulled him ever closer. It was sweet, wonderful heaven. His lips were soft and generous as he slowly began to unbutton her blouse. He lay relaxed in the hay, never taking his eyes from hers. She devoured the desire in his face. His lips moved hungrily across her skin and Ann felt an ecstasy she couldn't describe. She knew she wanted more, much more as he moaned and pulled her beneath him, pinning her under his great frame as he whispered endearments, obviously as carried away as she.

But when a subtle urgency began to enter into his words and gestures she suddenly realized she barely knew this man. In a flash she came to her senses, realizing she had let this go much too far. She pushed him from her, using all of the strength she could muster.

"No!" she said, shaking her head, her words coated with vehemence. "No!"

She pulled herself away. Bits of hay shook out of her hair and fell from her back. In one stark second of reality she saw how ludicrous this situation was and what a ridiculous, easy fool she was about to make of herself.

In the same moment Nathan obviously came to the same conclusion and Ann sensed him withdraw from her and assume another manner, another personality really, which effectively blocked out the man she had responded to only seconds before.

"Sorry about that," he said a little coldly. "Doesn't take much in a place like this in the middle of a storm to get carried away . . ."

As his voice trailed off, a flickering shadow of the inner man was still there. He looked away while Ann finished pulling herself together in disgusted silence. Yet, she felt her body continuing to radiate to his and insidious vibrations of urgent unfinished business surrounded both of them. She saw his fists clench as he stood one foot extended, shoulders sloped, with his back to her. She couldn't trust herself to speak. She decided it was best to just get out of there. As she neared the door he caught her by the arm and met her troubled gaze squarely. He searched her face. "I'll be there to pick you up about six Saturday night. I really want to do that," he said softly.

There was an earnest, almost pleading sincerity to his words which he buffered with a mischievous smile. It pierced Ann to the marrow of her bones, but did not alleviate her feelings. She pulled roughly away and went rushing to her car. She was incensed beyond words at both him and herself and yet . . . yet, it took a great deal of strength to leave and she knew she was in trouble, real trouble.

She jerked the car door open, knowing he was watching every move. She could picture the smile on his face and she cursed herself for making such a juvenile mistake. *There's nothing to do but bluff it through,* she seethed to herself as she continued to berate her impulsiveness.

She drove her car straight home, splashing water from puddles and spewing gravel from the muddy county roads in what seemed an appropriate accompaniment for her emotions. She had probably just blown her reputation, but then she could deal with that. Lord knows with her headstrong ways she'd had enough experience. That really wasn't the issue. Already she could feel tiny twinges of yearning and then she candidly acknowledged that she really wanted to see Nathan again and she knew that she would.

CHAPTER THREE

"No, no, no," she sighed, flinging yet another dress across the room.

Ann tore through her closet for what seemed like the hundredth time, trying to decide on just the right outfit for the dance. Since her last encounter with Nathan this choice had taken on an importance she had not experienced since adolescence. Slowly she pulled out an elegant, long silky sheath relieved by a provocative diagonal flounce at the hem and fluttery butterfly sleeves.

"Never," she said.

This was a round and square dance at the fairgrounds and all of her sophisticated evening attire was just not appropriate. Yet, she didn't want to be too casual and she did want to fulfill the image that Mr. Shuman obviously wanted her to impart. She had to look sleek and sophisticated, but totally in tune with this community.

It was something she wouldn't have given a thought to earlier, but now she truthfully admitted she had other considerations on her mind as well. As she pulled each dress out she tried to picture Nathan's reaction when he arrived to pick them up. She had a beautiful, long, romantic organdy sashed with a ribbon—appropriately homey in style.

"Nothing long," she said to herself in disgust as she remembered the fun and casualness of these affairs. Western, no. Ohio was not Texas. "Ah-ha," she said as her hand fell on an ultrachic outfit she had purchased just before leaving Chicago when Ohio was on her mind. It was a silky version of culottes with an Old World blouse and a beautifully ornate vest covered with embroidery. The very latest silhouette, with just the right touch of evening shimmeriness, appropriately casual with the split culottes ending at midcalf.

"I don't know what all the fuss is about," her mother said from the doorway, as Ann whirled around to greet her unexpected appearance, "but if you want my opinion, and you probably don't, I think folks around here would love that pretty full-circle skirt you've got hanging there with the matching shawl."

Ann looked at her mother and saw her twinkling calculating eyes. It was an excellent suggestion. With a low-necked long sleeve blouse and high-heeled strappy sandals, it would be a perfect casual but dressy outfit for the dance.

"Thanks, Mom," she said, smiling broadly. "That's a wonderful idea!"

As she looked at the other outfit again she realized it would be just a touch too exotic and would probably have branded her as a little too different, which was certainly not what she wanted to accomplish on her first outing in the community.

"I imagine you'll turn enough heads in that," her mother said with a mischievous smile, but it was obvious that she was both pleased and amazed that Ann had taken her advice.

Seeing her mother's pleasure, Ann felt marvelous and

realized that in truth she had resolved all her conflicts about both home and Jeff. In a startlingly short time she had come to feel very comfortable and close to both her parents. Her honest confrontation with her feelings about Jeff in the place where they had occurred had miraculously cleansed her of resentment and now she cherished in sweet but healthful sadness the memories and love they had shared. She would never have believed it would be so easy, yet common sense told her there was much to be said for time and its natural way of healing wounds once nature was allowed to take its course. The scars were there, but the pain was gone.

When her mother called her a few hours later she was just finishing the final touches to her appearance. She had heard Nathan's car come into the drive and her heart began to beat in a breathless nervous pattern. She tried to control it by taking deep breaths and busying her hands as she tied the shawl about her casually.

"Be right there," she called out gaily, exuding much more confidence than she felt.

She was suddenly in the grip of queasy shakiness as she uneasily recalled her last encounter with this perplexing but thoroughly challenging man. She had decided to act as if their tryst in the barn had never occurred.

As she came down the steps into the living room she knew immediately that her mother's choice of dress had been right. "Good evening," she said with a demure smile.

Nathan's eyes were like embers hiding behind his usual jocular facade. She felt them piercing through her as he perused her leisurely, taking in every detail of her appearance.

"Evening," he returned.

Although dressed casually in the spirit of the dance he

41

had a definite roguish air about him that was undeniably attractive. His short clipped hair was combed back with a fresh-washed look and an earthy male after-shave titillated her senses. A tweed jacket emphasized the breadth of his shoulders and chest, the stark white collar of his shirt contrasting boldly with the healthy golden hue of his complexion.

Ann could feel her parents watching them and she suddenly felt as though she were in the middle of a stage. At the same time she also became aware of two more pairs of eyes as Nathan moved to introduce her to his children.

"These are my kids, Tanya and Christopher," he said with casualness as he motioned to them. They moved forward to greet her a bit self-consciously. Both politely shook her hand, and Ann tried to help them feel at ease with a warm smile.

"You sure are pretty," her dad said as he came over and gave her a warm hug.

"That she is," said Nathan as he took her arm and they all began to move toward the door.

A warmth rushed through Ann as she looked at him from the corner of her eye. For some reason she hadn't anticipated that sort of response from him and it made her feel unexpectedly elated.

"Thank you," she said, as she struggled to retain a warmly polite demeanor.

His hand was like electricity on her inner arm and she could feel herself responding as visions of those few intimate moments in the hay came instantly to mind. She saw a sly little smile begin to play over his face and she knew he was remembering, too. She walked firmly through the door he held open and then warmly attached herself to Christopher as they walked toward the car. As it roared to life a moment later the group settled into friendly chatter. Ann's parents obviously enjoyed the company of the lively teen-agers as Mrs. Taylor quickly verified their ages of fourteen and fifteen and their status in school.

She and Nathan sat quietly next to each other, contributing a word or two to the friendly conversation. Yet there was a distinct and riveting bond uniting them as her thigh felt the outline of his burning through her thin skirt and the motion of his driving took constant advantage of the proximity of her breasts. His upper arm brushed casually again and again against hers. His crinkling mischievous eyes looked straight ahead, pausing every once in a while to glance covertly at her.

Ann was grateful for the darkness as she felt an insidious flush spreading throughout her body. She could feel her hair growing curlier as her brow grew moist. When Nathan surreptitiously cracked the window, allowing a small stream of cool air to flow over both of them, she felt an immense note of satisfaction. *It was a two-way street after all,* she thought to herself.

They rolled on through the country twilight toward the county fairgrounds. Tanya and Christopher had relaxed completely and seemed warmly impressed with Ann.

"I really like the perfume you're wearing," said Tanya.

She was a bright and vivacious girl with long, carefully coiffed hair, which indicated her expertise with both the blow dryer and curling iron. She was very attractively dressed in the latest high school fad, but she was obviously also very taken with Ann's sophisticated appearance.

Ann laughed and responded, "It's called 'Passion of the Senses,' " she said with theatrical emphasis.

"Oh, I love it," said Tanya.

"So do I," said Christopher, moving a little closer.

A tiny smile played about Nathan's lips as he noted his son's response. He too moved closer and took a deep breath of her scent, exhaling it in subtle satisfaction. Ann was genuinely amused as she thanked them for the compliment.

Christopher was the typical gangling fourteen-year-old, but he was undeniably attractive and had a winning personality which Ann was sure he used devastatingly on girls of his own age.

Within moments they were entering the fairgrounds, heading for the big hall where the dance was being held. It was years since Ann had been to a round and square dance, but she quickly responded to the lively chords of the country music coming across the way and the melodious sounds of the caller reciting the routine of a sprightly square dance. As they walked through the door into the noisy happy crowd, Mr. Shuman was there to greet them. They were soon immersed in the atmosphere of the event and Ann was having a wonderful time.

She was never without a partner, but Nathan seemed to take his role as escort very seriously as he came back time and time again and led her out onto the floor with him. He was a marvelous square dancer and easily led her through steps she had all but forgotten, but which seemed to come back more and more easily as the evening went on. It did not escape Ann's notice, however, that when she was dancing with someone else, Nathan never lacked for a partner and he flirtatiously encouraged all of the women who came near him. There was a laughing, relaxed casualness about him that was almost irresistible and he never lacked for attention.

Tanya and Christopher seemed to meet many friends there, but Ann was touched when she saw them dance together and when Nathan proudly escorted Tanya to the floor as his partner. Christopher paid Ann a great deal of attention, basking in the obvious bravery he was displaying by asking the honored guest to dance with him.

As the evening wore on, Nathan's embraces grew more and more familiar. When he whirled her around from an allemande left and then clutched her to him as they skipped around the circle, he molded his body to hers, his lips within centimeters of touching her flushed face as they laughed and responded to the outrageous chants of the caller.

Flushed and perspiring, he pulled her ever closer as the lights dimmed and the band slowed down into a slow romantic ballad. He expertly led her away in an easy ballroom step. Almost as if mesmerized he held her close while his lips traced her ear and they danced in silent communal wonder.

"You dance wonderfully," she sighed, as she pulled away to meet his eyes.

"Shh," he said and pulled her closer.

It was almost as if he wished not to be disturbed. As Ann felt her breasts responding to the hardness of his chest while his legs molded sensuously to hers, guiding her smoothly around the floor, she suddenly had a memory as a little girl when she had attended a dance such as this with her parents. She remembered seeing Nathan with his wife, Mona, who was his date at the time. They had danced just like this, beautifully and wonderfully together. In sinking realization she surmised he was using her in his own private fantasy. She pulled herself away roughly and met his startled eyes.

"It's warm," she said. "I think I need some air."

She turned and walked away. She was saddened when

he made no move to follow her. On the contrary, he turned quickly and soon had another partner in his arms continuing smoothly where he had left off with her.

"Cad," she seethed.

But as she quickly quelled her anger and hurt, it came to her in real comprehension that this was a little more complex than what she had anticipated. She had just resolved all of her own long-standing problems. She didn't need a whole new set now.

"Better leave well enough alone," she said with a sigh.

She was looking for an exit just as Mr. Shuman appeared next to her side. "Ann," he said, "I've been looking for you. I want to introduce you to all of these folks."

She felt herself being hustled onto the small stage platform where the band played. "Ladies and gentlemen," she heard him saying into the microphone, "I just want to take a moment to introduce you to Miss Ann Taylor, one of our own who has returned to her home community after working with Green Valley Farms as a specialist in public relations . . ."

Ann could feel all of the eyes in the room focusing on her and she felt the familiar boost of adrenaline, reminiscent of the many times she had addressed large crowds in the past few years. Almost as if attracted by a gravitational pull she felt her eyes drawn to Nathan's, his gaze boring through her while he hid behind a smiling face. He joined the others in clapping as the crowd responded to her introduction.

"Ann will be working throughout the county as an extension agent," Mr. Shuman went on, "and I thought it appropriate that we officially welcome her back tonight."

Ann smiled and took a deep breath. As the microphone enlarged and embellished her smooth, practiced voice she disengaged her inner self and continued to glance about the hazy room. She kept it short and charming, assuring everyone of her happiness in being back in the community along with a promise to serve them well.

While the phrases rolled through her smiling lips she noted Christopher speaking animatedly to a nice-looking man of about her own age. When she finished and enjoyed another round of applause, Christopher was speaking to the bandleader, who was nodding enthusiastically.

Many people came up to speak to her personally and the man who had been with Christopher earlier came over and introduced himself.

"Hello," he said affably, as he extended his hand. "I'm Dale Spencer, the music teacher at Christopher's school." He smiled broadly and Ann found herself smiling back. "You're about to hear one of my best students," he continued charmingly.

"Oh," said Ann, but before she could reply further she was engulfed by other well-wishers and she grew breathless with the exhilaration that such attention always creates.

There was some rearranging of the band on the platform and then to Ann's astonishment the bandleader stepped forward and introduced Christopher. Her eyes panned unconsciously around the room. She gasped when she saw Nathan standing alone. He was leaning against the wall in the back of the hall and his face was stony as the bandleader stepped back to accompany Christopher.

Ann was both amazed and impressed with Christopher's apparent resourcefulness and courage. She was even more amazed a few seconds later. The room grew hushed and still as Christopher's fingers became magic and turned the guitar into a simple singing symphony. She watched as he nimbly performed intricate runs and picked out a lively melody only to be further mesmerized when he stepped to the microphone and began to sing in a clear, talented voice.

She couldn't take her eyes from him. He was obviously a natural performer with a deep reservoir of talent. Ann was not a musical expert, but even a layman could see that special quality.

"Not bad, is he?" said a deep male voice behind her. Ann turned and met the grinning eyes of Dale Spencer.

He spoke with the special anticipation that comes so rarely to those of his profession, when they know they have discovered a real talent.

"He's wonderful," she smiled back. "Really. I wish you both every success—"

She was hustled away before he had a chance to respond, but she saw his quick genial smile of satisfaction and was really very glad she had met him.

She looked around the hall, searching for Nathan, anxious for some reason to see his response to his son's performance. She was aghast when she finally met his gaze. He hadn't moved an inch, but he stood ramrod straight, his powerful arms crossed in front of him in an angry clench. He was very angry. Every line of his body spoke of anger as he openly and defiantly glared at his son.

CHAPTER FOUR

The ride home from the dance had been very different from their earlier ride. There was an obvious tension in the car as Christopher glanced furtively at his father. Ann was appalled. Nathan had not in any way recognized Christopher's fantastic performance or uttered one word of praise. It was obvious that he was very displeased and Christopher was hurt.

Mrs. Taylor, ever perceptive, had done much to lighten the atmosphere and was outrageous in her praise of both Tanya and Christopher and the fun of the evening. Nathan just sat silently, glowering, and Ann could have cheerfully wrung his neck.

Stubborn, selfish man, she had thought.

After a while Nathan did begin to rally and his usual front of good humor seemingly returned as they neared home. He handed Ann out of the car with a resounding farewell laugh and then he, Tanya, and Christopher were all off with a happy chorus of good-byes. Ann decided it wasn't worthwhile to dwell on this family relationship. Tanya and Christopher were after all teen-agers and most families had their problems. She had no way of knowing what the real basis of the friction was and it was evident that this family also had abundant love. Ann, nevertheless, still found Nathan's response to his son's musical performance rankling.

Now she sat in Mr. Shuman's office, about to begin her first official day of work.

"Tell me about Nathan Warner," she said. "What is this big conflict he has?"

"Well, really, there isn't any real conflict," said Mr. Shuman, "except in Nathan's own mind. We're really in agreement with him about most things—"

"Well, then, what's the problem?"

Ann was clearly confused now.

"The problem is that Nathan can't see anyone else's point of view except his own. He fails to consider that he has advantages that most other farmers don't have. More than eight hundred acres of family homestead land free and clear and the benefits from several generations of good farmers. Almost every other farmer today, in addition to the usual risks, is mortgaged and fighting high interest rates to keep going. We try to provide reasonable guidance suitable for all of them."

"I still don't understand," said Ann. "Doesn't Nathan farm like everyone else?"

"No, not really," said Shuman. "You see, we all know that the most efficient and productive operation is the well-managed family farm. But since Nathan's wife died from cancer he's in some ways more of an environmentalist than a farmer. It makes him mad when you tell him that. He says he's a farmer the same as everyone else, but he won't use synthetic fertilizers, herbicides, and such. On the other hand some of his theories and practices are proving out and we're as interested in them as in any of the other latest scientific advances."

"So what is it, then?" asked Ann.

50

"He just refuses to compromise," said Shuman in final exasperation. "Whenever we bring out some new technology, especially when it comes to anything chemical, he just goes beserk."

"Well, why put up with it?" asked Ann.

"Because he's a valuable man and a good farmer who has a lot to contribute. He's a leader in the county, an expert in organic farming recognized statewide, *and,*" he said finally, "we're a public agency so that's our job. I was hoping," he said with a wink and a teasing smile, "you'd be able to get along with him. We know he has an eye for pretty ladies."

"Thanks a bunch," said Ann with a smile.

They went on with the conference. Nathan's name came up again as trustees of the county fair board were mentioned. As they wound up with discussion about the county fair, visions of the square dance came to mind. Ann remembered Christopher's remarkable performance and then she was once again reminded of Nathan's strange reaction to his son's obvious talent. It left her with a prickling, disturbed feeling as she went about organizing her new duties. While she shuffled papers and made phone calls tiny whispers of stolen intimate moments also hovered about and she knew she was treading in dangerous waters. Then she remembered her resolve to clear him from her thoughts.

In a totally unrelated turn of her mind she began thinking of the Harding farm. She reached for the telephone directory and called the real estate firm listed on the For Sale sign.

Almost unbelievably, three days later she was standing in the middle of the old farmyard again and she was honestly negotiating in an attempt to buy it. She had

51

gotten the owner to consider just the farmyard and five surrounding acres, which was all that she wanted. She was taking one final look and realized this was exactly the right place for her to start anew—a compromise with the past and present—and as a final flourish, she had decided to construct an underground house utilizing wind and solar power.

"An underground house!" her mother had exclaimed. "Why that sounds downright exciting. You know, of course, we'd love to have you here, daughter, but we know having a place of your own is important, too."

Ann was surprised by her mother. She had expected quite a different response.

"You know, there's a fellow in Zanesville, designs that kind of house," she said. "Maybe I can find his number . . . ."

"Wait, wait, Mom," said Ann, laughing. "I haven't bought the place yet."

"Oh, Lord a goshen, yes," her mother said. "I guess I'd better leave you to take care of your own things. Sometimes I just forget. . . ."

"Don't worry about it," said Ann, laughing. "I'm just glad you like the idea."

It was amazingly simple. Ann would never have believed it could be so simple. Just a matter of signing a few papers, of handing over a sizable amount of her savings, and the old Harding farmyard and surrounding five acres were hers.

She stood in the center of the weed-strewn yard and felt a wonderful sense of euphoria and satisfaction. She had made up her mind. She definitely was going to build an underground house. The architect would be there in just a few moments.

The weather had really warmed up in just a month and the balminess of May breezes along with the chatter of birds at home in a natural overgrown wilderness was wonderful. First priority was to leave as much of this intact as possible. She wanted big floor-to-ceiling windows someplace so she could watch and enjoy the birds year-round. She remembered that was one of the things she had missed most in the city. She was just beginning to dwell on this when she heard a strange noise.

She looked around and saw several large Holstein cows coming into the area. They were accompanied by a mean, snotty-looking young bull. Ann knew immediately that he was going to be trouble. He had a ring in his nose, but he swung his short, mean horns belligerently. He raised his snout and sniffed the air defiantly, as a great bellow rolled up from his deepest innards and sounded his battle cry. Ann stood stock-still as he began to paw the ground menacingly. This was bad. She was completely out in the open with no place to go and this was a young, quick bull.

She had no wish to attempt matador theatrics with him, but she stealthily tugged at the sweater flung over her shoulders. The bull knew she was there and he had her number as he pawed again and then began a charge in her direction. Ann's feet were riveted to the ground as she saw the pounding hooves of the snorting beast advancing. She couldn't move, not even to breathe, as he charged. She closed her eyes expecting the worst just as he swept by and smashed into her car, caving in the door. With angry bellows he smashed the small car again and again, his tail twitching in rhythm with his awesome muscles. In sheer incredulity she watched as the bull systematically continued to demolish her car until at last anger overcame her fear and she screamed while at the same time waving the sweater to scare him away.

Too late she realized she had made a terrible mistake, as the rampaging animal turned and his eyes calculated his new target. The car was little more than an appetizer for his innate rage as he turned toward this much more interesting target. Ann ran, but she knew she was no match for his full head of speed so she willed herself to stop and at the last possible moment feinted to one side as his horns wrenched the sweater from her hands. Fear formed great drops of perspiration on her brow as she breathlessly looked for a place to get out of the way. She was given a few seconds of reprieve, as the bull's rage obviously was without reason or specific target, and he ran on into the side of the old barn causing boards to fall about him. As the boards beat over him he shook them arrogantly off and once again stopped still, twitching only his tail, and sized her up.

The barn was her only chance. If she allowed him to charge toward her and waited until the last second before running straight to the barn in the opposite direction of the bull's charge she might be able to climb up into the old haymow. She stood with her hands over her chest trying to still her wildly beating heart as the animal came pounding toward her. She gripped the ground with her running shoes and thanked God she had worn them just as she could almost feel the hot breath of the animal.

With a scream she raced past the beast and scrambled for the heights of the old barn. She sat breathless, waiting for him to return and start to shake the old barn down, but it was refuge for the moment. She was gasping for air when she heard someone hollering.

"Sam! Sam! What in the hell are you doing?"

The bull had just made his first charge at the barn and Ann knew it would be only moments before it gave way. Tears of sheer relief came to her eyes as Nathan broke through the trees and came toward the bull. He had a long bull stick and as the bull turned he expertly reached out and snared the ring in the animal's nose. Almost miraculously the bull calmed down into a docile pussycat of an animal.

Ann could feel herself growing dizzy, as blood pounded through her body and the full realization of what had happened washed over her.

Christopher was behind his father and Nathan handed the bull over to him. "Here," he said. "Looks like Sam here has caused us some more trouble. Take him and the cows back and I'll try to find the hole where they got out."

Christopher quickly herded the animals together and within seconds the wild scene of moments before had become peaceful and bucolic as Nathan ably assisted his son. Ann felt a board snapping beneath her as Nathan came toward her.

"Are you all right?" he asked.

There was real concern in his voice.

"Yes . . ." she said unsteadily. "I think so. . . ."

"Here, let me help you down."

His arms came up and Ann gratefully and naturally fell into them as he swung her away from more falling boards.

"By golly, you seem to be a walking disaster as a country girl."

He grinned as his eyes danced merrily over her disheveled appearance.

"By God, you've got guts, though. I don't think I could have ever stood so long in front of a charging bull!"

"You saw it!" she said, instantly angry. "And you did nothing to help!"

"Couldn't reach you in time," he grinned. "And then I was afraid I would divert him the wrong way and spoil your escape."

His arms held her a little tighter as he hugged her in obvious praise of her courage. Ann realized she had remained in his arms, her hands pressed flat against his chest, as they talked. Her whole body was suddenly molten as she unconsciously responded to his intimate nearness. She sensed his breath quickening and knew he was having the same reaction. His voice dropped to more intimate cajoling as he continued with his teasing.

"I did save you, though, didn't I?"

His eyes met hers and she saw deep embers of desire igniting, as her hair whipped around her flushed and pouting face.

"I think I deserve something for that."

His lips came down on hers and seared her with a track of urgent fire as he melded her body to his. She could feel herself giving in far too easily and struggled to avoid a repeat of their earlier, intimate tryst in the barn.

"Owe you!" she seethed. "I don't owe you anything! That beast nearly demolished my car!"

"What?" Nathan gasped as he lifted his head and pulled back. "Oh, my God," he laughed as he began to walk around Ann's small compact car. As he examined it, he was literally overcome with laughter as great bellows bent him over double until Ann was sure tears were coming from his eyes. "That would have been something to see," he finally gasped, as another tide of laughter washed over him.

"I don't see anything at all funny about this," she said,

but in spite of herself she was finding his laughter infectious and suddenly the hilarity of the entire incident finally enveloped her. Before she knew it she was back in his arms in a comradely way. They both sat on the ground and laughed in utter abandon, almost as if sharing a mutual moment of release. Nathan's lips innocently and naturally began a soft nuzzling tract over her features and Ann felt the immediate teasing of a sensuous response. The laughter died and their eyes locked in expectant challenge.

Slowly Nathan rolled over her, laying her down gently in the pungent spring grass as he traced rays of warm sunlight that played over her face with one fingertip. Her lips parted and met the thrust of his tongue as he kissed her deeply. His arms pulled her close with an undeniable urgency. His lips sent a track of fire down her neck and sent shivers through her from head to toe. Ann pulled him closer, tousling his hair and reveled in the feel of his intense embrace. It was ethereal and sweet and she yearned for more. Her lips met his again and his hand cupped and caressed her breast then moved to tug urgently at the buttons of her blouse. They both paused when they heard a car coming slowly up the road. A mischievous glint lit up his eyes as Nathan surveyed their surroundings.

"You know," he said with an affected grimace, "if we're going to make a habit of this maybe we ought to plan these things a little better."

Reality surfaced and Ann knew she had made another strategic mistake. She was immediately angry as she fought both the rampaging response of her body and his infuriating candor. "I'm not making a habit of anything!" she spit out. She scrambled up and brushed herself off, giving angry emphasis to her words.

"You might have fooled me," he said with drawling theatrics. "Frankly, I've never been one to refuse a direct invitation."

"You beast," she said.

She turned as she heard wheels coming in the short lane to the farmyard. She whirled around as the car of J. Randolph Cooper came into view. He unfolded his six-foot-plus frame, which boasted rangy, relaxed good looks, and she went to greet him.

"Well," said Nathan, "I see Sam was disturbing more than I imagined. . . ."

"Just mind your own business," she said in low guttural tones. She was angry, embarrassed, and hurt beyond the point of speaking to him civilly.

"That I will," he said as the cold shade came down over his face. He grabbed his hat and pulled it angrily over his brow, giving him a menacing look. "I'll see to your car," he said. "Send me the bill."

He turned on his heel and walked away, yet as Ann watched him, a caldron of seething emotions herself, she noted a dejected hunch to his shoulders and found herself wanting to run after him in spite of her anger.

"Miss Taylor, I presume."

Ann turned around and confronted the smiling face of the architect her mother had suggested. He extended his hand and in relief Ann greeted him warmly as Nathan disappeared through the surrounding woods. She found herself looking into friendly blue eyes, and as he reached to calm his burnished blond hair, she felt an immediate rapport with him.

"I had a devil of a time finding this place, but it's lovely. Perfect for an underground house."

He spoke with an unusual, cultured British accent.

"Yes," said Ann, smiling to him, although she was still a little shaky.

She noted him watching Nathan's retreat.

"I hope I'm not interrupting anything," he said, consciously polite but inquisitive at the same time.

"No, no," she said, as she regained her full composure and was suddenly overcome again with the hilarity of her earlier situation. "Actually I've just been chased by a bull that belongs to Nathan Warner there and in the process had my car practically demolished—"

"I say, you have," he said, noticing the condition of her car. "Are you sure you want to go on with this now? Perhaps I should help you take care of your car."

"Well, you can probably give me a lift when we're through, but you're here now, so let's talk about the house."

She felt a sense of heady anticipation at the very thought of actually going through with her plans, which had seemed little more than a gossamer dream until this very moment. Now she realized it had every possibility of becoming a reality.

"I understand you're a well-known pioneer in this type of house," she said. "Obviously, though, you're not from around here."

"No," he said, laughing. "I'm from Australia. I came here as an exchange student some years ago and just never really got back. I received a grant and fellowship, finally apprenticing with a large architectural firm. One thing has just led to another. Now I'm completely involved with this housing concept."

"Great," said Ann, as they began walking over the site. But as they talked she could still see Nathan walking away in her inner mind and she wondered why she continued to allow herself to be exposed to such an outrageous, gauche, insulting man. Randolph was a very attractive man, perhaps younger than she, but most definitely attractive and charming. Dale Spencer was a nice man. Why couldn't she be sensuously fascinated with a nice man?

She wondered if she was responding to some inner, self-destructive urge and made an agreement with herself to examine this thoroughly. In the meantime she was disturbed by Nathan. She ran her fingers unconsciously over her face, where only moments before his lips had left a track of fire.

CHAPTER FIVE

Randolph was a joy to work with and within a short time Ann had not only a preliminary set of plans for her underground house, but a delightful camaraderie as well with a man who, she admitted, reminded her in some ways of her brother Jeff. They were becoming good friends. She knew that was probably the extent of it, yet there was something decidedly dashing about him. . . . If only something about Nathan Warner would quit nagging at her.

Now she sat looking at a message from Dale Spencer. He was a nice man, unattached, as it turned out, and Ann had had several enjoyable outings with him as well as with Randolph, but in his case there was definitely no fireworks. Just warm understanding and comfortable friendship, for which she was grateful. In spite of her better judgment her thoughts insisted upon revolving around Nathan, riveted by the challenge of his mystery and his chameleon facades.

She hadn't heard from him directly since the escapade with the bull. He had inquired about the repair bill for her car by calling the garage and then he went by and paid for the damage. All in all, it was a rather unsatisfactory conclusion.

Ann had the distinct feeling that he was avoiding her.

She could almost sense his embarrassment. He had by now surely learned of her purchase of the land which coincidentally bordered his own, thus explaining the rampaging cows, but she had never heard the first word from him, let alone an apology for his behavior. It bothered her and left her with a funny empty feeling. Although she was actively encouraging other romantic diversions and continued to insist adamantly to herself that, aside from an obvious physical attraction, she and Nathan were hardly suited for each other anyway, she decided she had to find a way to reach him, to talk with him. She hoped to find a way that was not too obvious.

In a moment of sheer calculation—she was too honest to label it anything else—she picked up the phone and called the Warner number, asking to speak to Tanya. Christopher answered the phone and was delighted that Ann had called. She could hear background noises as the receiver hung in limbo until Tanya arrived. Ann's heart was suddenly beating erratically, but she willed her voice to stay calm as she spoke into the receiver.

"Tanya?" she said, a lilt in her voice. "I was wondering if I could get you to help me with a project for the Lost Arts Festival."

"Sure," the young girl replied. "What do you have in mind?"

Within moments Ann had made arrangements to meet with Tanya at the Warner house later in the afternoon. *It really was a stroke of genius,* she thought smugly to herself.

Every year Pataskala had a Lost Arts Festival and she had by accident come upon some very strange-looking utensils in her mother's kitchen, only to learn that they were remnants of many commonly used kitchen tools of the past century or so. In many instances she couldn't guess their function. Once informed, though, she found their uses quite obvious. They had become obsolete because of more modern appliances and the increasing use of processed foods in the home. They were quaint and interesting and she knew such a collection along with a demonstration of their uses would be a wonderful project for the festival, while also preparing an excellent foundation for her future plans.

The Warner house, like her parents', was one of the few remaining old houses in the area that had belonged continuously to the same family, so she was sure there was a veritable treasure of such artifacts secreted away in the old cupboards and attic. Tanya was, therefore, an excellent choice for an assistant and it would, Ann candidly admitted, allow her the chance she wanted to confront Nathan on more or less neutral territory.

She realized with a start that her sense of smug satisfaction was really a little ludicrous just as Dale Spencer came through the door of her small cubicle of an office.

"Dale," she said, genuinely glad to see him. "I just got your message that you'd be stopping by—"

"Yes," he said a little hesitantly, sitting down across from her and acknowledging the slip of paper in her hand. "I'm hoping you might be able to help me with something."

"Sure, if I can," she said.

"Well," he said, as he took a deep breath and obviously decided to just plunge in. "You know, other than at the dance a few weeks ago I've never said too much to you about Christopher Warner, but I think you can see that he's very talented . . ."

He seemed to be searching for words.

Ann waited patiently, as she wondered what this was all about.

"You know, he has little or no encouragement from home," he said with a little grimace. "And you've probably heard that his father has this fixation about Christopher carrying on the family farming tradition. Nathan Warner is a very stubborn man."

"No, I didn't know why Nathan was so negative," she said, "but it was rather obvious at the dance. I was puzzled about that."

"Well, Christopher really should have been studying seriously years ago," Dale continued, "but Nathan wouldn't hear of private lessons. Then a year ago Nathan finally agreed that Christopher's free time is his own. Since then he's spent every spare moment in lessons and rehearsals and paid his own way."

"Well then?" said Ann.

She was clearly confused now as Dale went on.

"Christopher and I have had some very serious discussions, and along with his talent he's very resourceful and recognizes an opportunity when he sees one. He'd like to take part in a special competition this year and . . ."

Dale squirmed ever so slightly as he looked at her with another little grimace.

"To make a long story short," he sighed, "Christopher knows that will really be pushing his dad . . ."

"Yes," said Ann a little exasperated, "but I don't understand—"

"Why I'm discussing this with you," Dale broke in. "Well, the reason is that Christopher admires you very much." Dale took a deep breath and then rushed on bluntly. "He thinks you might be able to help him reach his father."

"What!" she gasped. "Why, I hardly know them . . . I don't see what I could . . ." *If only he knew,* she thought to herself while she groped for words. As she thought of her current estrangement from Nathan she was completely flabbergasted by this suggestion.

"I know," said Dale, breaking in again, "and you're probably wondering why *I'm* not talking to Nathan."

"No, no," said Ann. "Under the circumstances I can certainly understand your position. It's just that . . ."

Ann could feel herself growing irritated with Nathan again. Why did he have to be such a narrow-minded, unreasonable person?

"I know what you're thinking," Dale continued, "but in spite of this rather bleak picture we're painting of Nathan and Christopher's relationship, there is a genuine bond of love in that family. Nathan just seems to have a blind spot about this, but fortunately Christopher seems to understand it. He's not in any way disrespectful, but neither is he intimidated or inhibited. He'd just like to have some additional moral support. He thought you'd make a great ally . . ."

"And if Nathan is unhappy with this?"

"Well, I'll be honest with you. Nathan hasn't taken this too seriously yet. That's what Christopher's hoping you'll help him with . . ."

Great, thought Ann to herself.

She had just moments before taxed her brain to think of some way to reach Nathan, hoping for some reconciliation of their spirits and understanding of each other. Mr. Shuman had more or less appointed her their goodwill ambassador so far as Nathan was concerned. If she agreed to become involved with this she knew exactly what was going to happen. She could sense an impending disaster.

Yet the thought of Christopher trying so valiantly to please everyone, while at the same time not giving full vent to his own innermost needs, was a situation she couldn't legitimately ignore.

"Well, I don't know what I can do," she said at last, "but certainly if the opportunity arises I suppose I could speak to Nathan. If Christopher honestly feels he can manage this I think he ought to be encouraged. This won't interfere with his other studies or chores, will it?"

"No, of course not," Dale replied. "He'll have very little free time, but you see, in many ways, Christopher is like his father with a natural talent for management. He has a maturity that is amazing, balanced by the most fiendish juvenile sense of humor you can imagine. He knows exactly what he's doing."

"That's great," said Ann in finality, "and I'll be looking forward to attending the competition."

"You bet," said Dale as he arose to leave.

When he made his exit Ann knew she might have just laid the groundwork for a smoldering confrontation. Actually she didn't know Nathan that well, but she had seen his face and experienced his glowering disapproval the night of the dance. But then she did feel Christopher had a right to pursue his own goals and there was really no reason why she should be involved unless a chance conversation offered the opportunity of a positive result. Certainly there was no reason to pursue this aggressively and leave herself wide open for all of Nathan's churlish displeasure. She assured herself of this firmly.

Nevertheless, as she reached for her sweater in preparation for her date with Tanya, all of her earlier scheming took on a different cast. She almost hoped now that she wouldn't encounter Nathan during the visit. She nearly called and canceled her appointment, but faltered at the last moment, feeling that was cowardly.

An hour later when she pulled into the Warner drive, Tanya came to greet her from the barn. Ann smiled, remembering her own youth when she spent more time in the barn than the house. Tanya waved and came up smiling as Ann emerged from the car. Although the better part of June was gone, she reveled in the glory of late spring as the aroma of roses and grass mingled with the other farmyard smells.

"Hi," said Tanya. "Be with you in just a second. Dad will be in soon. After supper I may go out and help him finish up the last of the field work."

There was a sparkle in her eyes and voice. Ann could see that there was no resentment, only a sincere eagerness.

"Sounds like you really love your work," said Ann.

"Oh, yeah," said Tanya a little sheepishly. "It's always so exciting in the spring when you're rushing to get the crops in and everything is clean and fresh. It's so much fun to plan and then watch the crops come up. Not so much when you have to worry about the weather and all of that, but then that's kind of what makes it exciting, too."

Ann looked at Tanya astutely and remembered her own youth. She had always loved working with the animals, but the field work had never impressed her very much.

"You're a real farmer then, aren't you?"

She laughed as she put her arm comfortably around the young girl's shoulders.

"I sure am," she said. "I'm planning to go to agriculture school at Ohio State and I've told Dad I'll run this place one day just as well as he does."

Ann looked at the young girl's radiant face and realized she had just gained a startling insight.

"What does your dad think of all that?" she asked softly.

"Well, to tell you the truth," said Tanya, "he's a little bit of a chauvinist when it comes to that. I love him and want to be just like him, but he seems to think that Christopher should be the one to run the farm because I'll get married and have babies and all that stuff. But I've told him I'm going to stay right here and live in this house and farm this farm until the day I die. He just laughs, but he'll see. Christopher loves the farm, but he wants to do other things, too."

At the mention of Christopher, Ann could feel herself beginning to blush, but she was also amazed at Tanya's candor. It was typical of adolescence, but again, while she spoke critically of her father, Tanya's statements were more affectionate than resentful.

As they entered the farmhouse the wonderful yeasty aroma of rising bread met them.

"My word, you have been busy this afternoon," said Ann appreciatively. "That bread smells wonderful."

"Oh, I'm not doing that. That's Christopher. We're having a contest this week to see who makes the best bread. I bake to humor Dad, but Christopher loves it. Between his cooking and music it's a good thing he chases the girls or Dad would be out of his gourd over him."

"Who'd be out of his gourd?" asked Christopher, coming in.

He was laughing and met Ann with obvious delight, but he seemed to be a little uncharacteristically shy, too.

"How's this for perfect management? I've timed this so that the rising of the bread was done at the same time I finished the barn and garden chores."

Ann had the distinct feeling that he knew she had just

spoken with Dale Spencer, but decided not to mention it. She wanted a little more time to think this through. He was still grinning as he went to the sink to wash his hands and as Ann and Tanya continued on into the living room. He was soon busy shaping the dough into loaves. Ann heard other pots and pans rattling a little later on and realized he was preparing dinner, too.

She shook her head and smiled. It was impossible not to feel both affection and admiration for these kids. It was also refreshing to hear respect in their voices when conversing with and about adults. Although they were impish it was obvious that they had had a good basic foundation in decency. Ann realized most of this must have come from Nathan and thought perhaps her instincts were not totally wrong. Although he was obviously stubborn, there *was* a man worth knowing beneath all of that hayseed nonsense.

As the word stubborn came to mind, supported by Tanya's revelations, Ann had a sinking feeling about her earlier conversation with Dale Spencer. *Well, no matter,* she thought resolutely, Nathan was not the only one who could be stubborn and she was not going to allow him to intimidate her when she knew she was doing the right thing.

She set her chin firmly as Tanya led her into a small sunny sitting room just off the big kitchen. She was greeted by older version of Nathan as he sat resting in a big rocker.

"Hi, Grandpa," said Tanya, giving him a kiss. "This is Ann Taylor. You probably know her. She used to live around here."

"Why, I surely do," he said, rising with obvious delight

in his eyes. "All grown up and pretty, too. Whatever brings you here?"

He motioned both of them to sit down.

"She works at the county extension office," said Tanya, a little louder than normal, "and she's asked me to help her with a project for the Lost Arts Festival."

"Well, I'll be," he said, as Ann quickly filled in the details of the project to both of them.

Grandpa Warner's eyes immediately lit up. "Why, there's dozens of things you can use here," he said in enthusiasm. "Take her up to the attic, Tanya. There's even an old trunk up there, belonged to a great aunt of mine. She and her husband were missionaries in China or some-place. She had to take everything she needed along with her and a lot of it was shipped back with their belongings when they got killed in a boat accident or something. I don't think anyone's looked through it in years."

"That sounds wonderful," said Ann. "Are you sure you don't mind?"

"Not at all," he said with a smile. " 'Bout time someone got some use out of all that junk up there."

"We've got some weird things right here in the kitchen drawers," said Christopher, as he came in wiping flour from his hands. He held a small round wooden mold with an ornate design, which Ann recognized as an old butter press, and a small metal container with a screw top and chain, used to make tea.

Ann smiled as she reached for his treasures, but Tanya admonished him.

"Christopher," she said with irritation. "You're getting flour all over everything. He can cook," she said wryly, "but he's a lousy housekeeper. Can't tell the difference between the barn and the house."

"You should talk," said Christopher as he retreated, just barely dodging the pillow Tanya threw at him.

Everyone was still laughing over their good-natured horseplay as Tanya and Ann trudged up the stairs to the attic. It was a cavernous room which ran the entire length of the house, lit by one bare lightbulb. Within moments both women were engrossed with their finds. Ann could feel a warm bond growing as Tanya rummaged through old boxes and picked up lanterns and buckets. They collapsed into laughter as they tried again and again to guess the uses of some of the things they found.

The light was growing dim when they finally found the trunk which Grandpa Warner had mentioned. They opened it and Ann saw immediately that it was a real find. Not only were there utensils and gadgets, but there were also bundles of letters, an old Bible, and some Oriental-looking keepsakes. Tanya set a beautiful exotic doll aside and began busily examining the tiny cups of a delicate tea set. Ann was gingerly handling what seemed to be a classical Oriental vase. She knew immediately that it was very old and something was just beginning to prick her mind when they heard a heavy crunch on the steps. Nathan came through the small door of the attic. His large frame was almost formidable, but his easy smile as he noticed the laughing rapport of Ann and his daughter put them at ease.

"Tanya," he said, as he gave his daughter a teasing smile, "I'm glad to see you're finally taking an interest in dolls and dishes."

Tanya threw him a funny look as the smile disappeared from her face.

Ann found herself suddenly swallowing with some difficulty and realized she had, indeed, been dreading seeing

71

him again since her meeting with the music teacher. She also had a sudden insight—she had been hoping her attraction to Randolph and other recent social diversions would have dulled her wild response to him. Sinkingly she knew it was not to be as a familiar weakness enveloped her body. She nevertheless smiled brightly as she greeted him warmly.

"Hello, Nathan," she said.

Nathan responded with a warm smile. Then he quickly began conversing about their activity as though nothing unpleasant had occurred just a few weeks before. His eyes, however, bored into her own and she could feel a vibrating communication.

Ann brushed her hair back, feeling a bit awkward. "We've just found this interesting trunk which your father mentioned, but it's getting dark and I was just thinking maybe we should look at it another day."

She was still holding the vase which to the untrained eye might seem like some gaudy Oriental bric-a-brac, but Ann admired the whimsical butterflies and flowers in its hand-painted design and sensed something very special about it. She returned it carefully to the trunk.

Nathan had watched her actions with interest.

"Well, you're welcome to come back anytime," he said, "but if you're really interested in that old trunk I'll bring it downstairs and you can take it with you. Take all the time you want with it. Seem's the least I can do after Sam chased you the other day."

He looked down at the floor a bit awkwardly and Ann realized she had just been apologized to. Although it was artless and roundabout, to say the least, it left her with a warm feeling as her eyes met his and they both smiled in understanding. Tanya was completely silent as she watched Ann with a growing wariness. She shrank away from the dishes and doll as Ann repacked them.

With easy strides Nathan came across the room and picked up the trunk. His muscles strained through his chambray work shirt. His tight jeans outlined his strong thighs and legs as he balanced the clumsy load and then began to move effortlessly toward the steps.

As Ann watched his athletic body she felt a familiar shaky response. She smiled at Tanya as they moved to follow Nathan and had a feeling that some of Tanya's enthusiasm for the project had dwindled. She was, however, so relieved over Nathan's relaxed attitude that she had little time to dwell on it.

When they emerged into the sitting room Nathan set the trunk down and continued his conversation with Ann in the same easy manner.

"I didn't realize when I saw you the other day that you'd bought part of the Harding farm. I hear you're planning to build an underground house."

There was a continued unspoken directive—more than a plea—for understanding underlining his words that should have annoyed her, but then it was rather awkward to come out in front of your kids and apologize for making unreasonable accusations.

There was the telephone, though, Ann thought. *He could have called. . . .*

Nathan motioned her to a comfortable chair as he continued with his conversation. "I've had my eye on that farm for some time," he said genially. "I'm glad you only took part of it . . ."

His eyes met hers and Ann felt a sense of warm, intimate camaraderie, but she submerged her thoughts as she spoke.

"Well," she said, "I just wanted enough land to build my house."

"I wish you luck with it," said Nathan. "I may just decide to make an offer on the rest of that place. Then you'll practically be surrounded by us as your neighbors."

He smiled.

"That's fine," said Ann. "Just as long," she added teasingly, "as you keep Sam on your side of the fence."

"That we'll try to do," said Nathan jokingly, as Tanya and Grandpa Warner joined in with the teasing that followed the recounting of that escapade.

"We'll be going back to the fields after supper," said Nathan, "but Christopher has been cooking up a storm out there since you arrived. I'm sure he'll be disappointed if you don't stay and eat with us."

She smiled.

"I'd be delighted," she said sincerely.

She enjoyed a happy, gregarious meal with all of them. Then, as she moved to leave, Nathan shouldered the trunk and carried it easily to her car as Christopher and Tanya both started for tractors to continue the last of the field work.

"I want you to know," he said suddenly, out of the blue, "I'm sorry. . . ."

Ann was confused for just a second.

He stood up from depositing the trunk in the back of her car. They were out of earshot from everyone else and his eyes looked deeply into hers. A smile warmed his rugged features.

"I was out of line the other day and I want you to know I really appreciate your interest in both Tanya and Christopher. . . . I . . . I, ah . . . know I've acted like a jerk a time or two and, well . . . I'd like to make it up by taking you to dinner. How about Saturday night?"

Ann was touched beyond words by this unexpected apology from him and her heart sank as she realized she already had plans for Saturday night.

"Well, actually, I've already made arrangements to meet with the architect for my house that night," she said. "He's coming all the way from Zanesville and . . ."

"That the fellow you were meeting the other day?"

She nodded.

"Okay," said Nathan much too quickly. She saw the shade come down and fall firmly into place as his eyes grew cold. "It was just a thought," he shrugged.

"Well, how about another night, Sunday, maybe?"

"No . . . let's just leave it," he said tightly. "What with all the work we have to do now it probably wasn't a very good idea, anyway."

"Any way you want it," said Ann through her own tight lips, as the warm rapport they had enjoyed just moments before disintegrated. "It was your idea in the first place!"

She really was getting a little tired of this difficult, intolerant man. Enough was enough. It was ridiculous to waste any more time on him. Going out with Randolph would at least be enjoyable. She turned to get into the car just as Grandpa Warner emerged from the house.

"Say," he called to Ann, "you almost forgot this. The kids put a bunch of those old things into a box for you, but you come back again. There's a lot of things I can tell you about."

His eyes were sparkling with enthusiasm and anticipation. Ann's heart went out to this feisty old man.

"You come back and visit," he said resoundingly.

"Yes," said Nathan softly, "come back."

Ann's head snapped up.

She instinctively knew she was talking to the real Nathan Warner as the shade lifted and she saw a plea for true understanding. She saw him visibly struggling with something she couldn't identify.

"I'll call you and we'll talk," he said, giving her car two little raps.

There was just a hint of a scowl on his face, but Ann felt inexplicably much happier with that expression than with the mischievous smile he so often displayed and hid behind.

She drove out of the lane and realized she may have just truly touched the real Nathan Warner for the first time since that first poignant meeting in the cemetery. It made her feel very good, but she wondered if he would ever really see her and not think of someone else. . . .

CHAPTER SIX

The next few days were like a reverie for Ann. She basked in the warmth of Nathan's farewell words. In the interval she seemed to float, alternately pleased with this turn of events, and then uneasy when she didn't hear from him, wondering if she had actually imagined the entire episode.

Although it was Saturday morning she had gotten up early. She really enjoyed the dewiness and warmth of the country early mornings. She was scheduled to tape a television interview that afternoon for a popular panel show. When she arose she had carefully examined her face, frowning as she discovered another tiny laugh line around her lips. Knowing that close television camera scrutiny has a tendency to be unkind to the ravages of time, her vanity ordained that she take special pains for this appearance.

She pushed her hair back with a wide band and then scrubbed her face vigorously. She routinely followed all of the usual beauty regimens, taking special pains with her manicures, adhering to the usual practices of relaxing baths, facials, and creams, but this line looked really serious. She frowned and then remembered she had just the thing for it.

She scrambled downstairs and found the briefcase she

had dropped next to the large rolltop desk in the small bedroom her mother had turned into a den. Quickly she found the instructions for a homemade facial to combat dry summer skin.

"Just what I need," she said, as she fingered the offending line.

She went into the large old-fashioned bathroom adjacent to the big screened-in porch. Although it was very early by city standards, Ann's parents were both up and gone. As she looked out the window she could see faraway thunderclouds in an angry sky. It looked as if it was going to be one of those days when any plans for field work would be a gamble.

She read over the instructions for the mask and quickly gathered cheesecloth and distilled water from her mother's laundry area. She checked the medicine cabinet and *voila*, found a bottle of rose water. The instructions said to soak the cheesecloth in those two ingredients and arrange it over the face for ten minutes while lying down with head hanging slightly over the edge of a bed. While doing this it was also suggested that you lift one leg at a time, slowly flex, point, and then gently rotate the foot.

"What does that have to do with dry skin?" she asked out loud. Oh well, if you were going to test something you had to follow all of the instructions.

After the mask a moisturizer was to be applied. Ann saw that a bottle of her usual brand was also there in the bathroom. The screen porch with rockers and one old Victorian chaise longue looked so inviting that she decided to carry out her beauty experiment right there.

She was soon settled on the chaise longue, cheesecloth in place, head hanging over the edge, feet flexing, rotating, and pointing, giving her the appearance of an animated mummy. She was about halfway through when she heard a step outside the porch door.

"That you, Dad?" she called.

"No," said a deep voice, which was obviously puzzled, but also held a hint of laughter. "Do you need some help?"

Ann was very discreetly covered in tailored silk pajamas, but that was all she had on and the pant legs had fallen loosely about her thighs displaying her shapely tanned legs as she went on with her exercise gyrations. She sat up quickly and met Nathan's amused eyes.

"Nathan! Whatever in the world are you doing here?" she asked in acute embarrassment.

Although there was a teasing grin on his face he looked away, uncomfortable for just a second. "Well, actually I had intended to say I'd come over to see your dad about a part I need for my tractor, but I guess I really was hoping to see you."

Ann looked at him in real surprise. He looked as though he had not slept well. His hair was still tousled and it appeared as though he was just barely pulled together. However, even in his rugged clothes, he was a pillar of strength and she felt his magnetism beginning to envelop her. It was all the more enticing coupled with his obvious vulnerability.

She sat up and self-consciously folded her arms across her breasts as the cheesecloth fell to the floor. Unable to resist the hilarity of her appearance, Nathan began to laugh. "What in God's name are you doing to yourself?" he asked.

"Making myself beautiful," she said, as she also acquiesced to the humor of the situation.

"Aren't you beautiful enough already?" said Nathan,

clearly amused. "Don't you have enough men panting after you now, including fools like me?"

Ann's laughing retort died on her lips as she looked straight through his teasing facade to the naked inner man. "What do you mean, a fool like you?" she asked softly.

She went to him and turned him about, forcing him to look at her directly. She could see the bluster draining from him, replaced by confused yearning. She reached up and lightly touched his face and began to trace its rugged planes as his eyes met hers. The wind from the storm ruffled their hair and punctuated the pathos of their emotions, as leaves and branches swirled around them.

"I . . . I want you, but I can't love you," he said. "And that's wrong. . . . I know that's wrong, but the funny thing is, it never seemed wrong before. . . . Just with you. . . ."

"I see," she sighed. "Maybe then, that's something we should talk about."

She looked about, realizing her parents might return at any moment. *Damn,* she thought. She slid her hands self-consciously over her sleeping attire.

"Look," she said hesitantly, not really wanting to leave him for an instant, "let me get some clothes on and let's have a cup of coffee."

Her eyes locked with his and with all the strength of her spirit she pleaded with him not to waver. He returned her gaze for what semed eons and then smiled.

"I'll make the coffee," he said.

She gave him a radiant smile and quickly sprinted up the stairs. In a flash she pulled on jeans and a loose shirt, leaving her feet bare. The kitchen was ominously dark when she returned as the clouds closed in steadily. She was reminded of the storm when they had been in the barn and she was suddenly self-conscious.

"I passed your mom and dad on the way over," he said a little sheepishly. "I really do need a part for my tractor and thought your dad might have a spare, but somehow I just seemed to come on."

Ann met his eyes again and relaxed immediately. This was a sincere man who was searching and exploring. The atmosphere was laden with tenderness. It was the moment she had been waiting for.

"Where do you keep the cups?" asked Nathan, opening cupboard doors.

"In here," she said.

She opened the door next to him and was immediately aware of his nearness when her arm brushed his.

"Uhmm, you smell good," he said, "like roses, all shiny and full of sunshine."

"Oh, go on with you," she said, blushing.

She ran her hands over her crumpled clothes and fluffed her hair with a familiar motion. Her fingers snarled in the wide band in her hair.

"Oh, my gosh! Now I've ruined my facial! Be back in a minute," she said as she raced out to get the moisturizer.

Shaking his head, Nathan laughed quietly. He set the steaming cups down and pulled out a chair opposite hers.

"After all that trouble, I have to do this anyway," she said as she began to apply the lotion vigorously to her face.

Nathan smiled as he continued to gaze at her in fascination.

In some mad way they were both settled and relaxed, a natural rapport emerging. They began to talk. It was almost as if they routinely began every day this way. Easy and familiar.

"That day I saw you in the cemetery," he said. "You were hurting—almost as much as I was. . . ."

"Yes," she said. "I was angry for so long and finally I guess I was finding a way to let it go."

"Your brother, Jeff?"

She nodded.

"I don't think I'll ever get over Mona," he said. "I think you need to know that right up front."

"No one ever does," she said. "And no matter how much you wish you could, you can't go back and change the past."

Their eyes locked again and Ann could feel the faint stirrings of her familar response to him.

"I don't think I could ever love anyone but Mona," he said, as he rubbed his neck and sighed. "But yet . . . I'm a man . . . I need certain things. Sometimes it's like maybe if I play my cards right, for just a moment I can touch her or see her again, but with you it's different."

"Different?"

"Yes, different. I don't know. Sometimes it's almost as if I'm forgetting. . . . It's not right. I . . . I feel . . ."

He groped for words.

"Guilty," said Ann. "You feel guilty."

"Yes. Guilty both ways. You've got me coming and going."

"Nathan, listen," Ann said, suddenly sure she wanted to reach this man more than anything she had ever wanted. "There's nothing wrong with your memory. It's something that belongs to you to cherish forever, but because of the love you had together I can't believe Mona would want you to live without affection for the rest of your life."

She got up and walked around the table. She reached for his hands and searched his face.

"Something about you has touched me," she said. "I'm not sure what it is exactly . . . but I'm here to stay. We both have things to work out and we have all the time in the world to explore our feelings. Maybe in the end we'll just be friends . . ."

"No, I don't think so," he said.

She could feel her heart beginning to race. Something told her not to let him go. Tires were crunching and popping up the driveway.

"Let's take a walk," she said softly.

He looked out the window.

"Sure," he said. "The storm seems to be passing."

They were out the door and starting across the field before her parents entered the house. She and Nathan walked in silence for nearly five minutes.

"You know," he finally said, as they trampled over the rough ground, "sometimes I just get so angry. I mean downright mad. . . . We had everything. I could almost tell you what she was thinking from one minute to the next . . . and . . . I just don't know why. Why? We never did anything to anyone!"

There was a severe look of exasperation and annoyance on his face. Ann turned and searched his face again. Somehow she knew this was a therapy that had been long in coming. All he needed was someone to listen. She stared ahead to the grove that loomed in front of them and kept on walking. Nathan had quickened the pace to suit the agitation of his words and she found herself growing a little breathless. He scowled and looked away.

"It just makes me so damned mad sometimes. When I look at this land and all that it promised us and somehow in our greed we just screwed it up and then Mona who never hurt anyone was taken . . ."

"Now just a moment," said Ann with just a touch of sternness in her voice. "Stop torturing yourself trying to understand. It just doesn't work that way. Nobody really knows what it's all about. The only thing you know for sure is that it happened."

He looked at her with a grimace. She knew she wasn't reaching him.

"Nathan," she said, as she stopped and forcefully grabbed his upper arms and turned him towards her. "It's all right to hurt. . . . Go on and hurt. That's between you and your own soul, but for God's sake don't destroy yourself, too. You don't have to dry up and blow away. That's not what it's all about. That's not right."

She could feel tears moistening her eyes as the wind whipped her hair around, but she riveted her eyes to him and forced him to meet the extension of her feelings. Slowly she felt him begin to soften as his angry rigidity began to dissolve and his eyes met hers in sweet, liquid communion. She felt as though her entire body was being buffeted about by the last swirls of the threatening storm, but she held her gaze steady and was at last rewarded with a tiny smile that played about his lips.

She put her arm around his back and fit snugly into his shoulder as they continued to walk on toward the grove. She remembered that it had been one of her favorite places when she was growing up. It was dissected by a winding creek and turned into an island by the property fence lines. She had always felt incredibly safe and peaceful there, completely isolated from the rest of the world.

His arm came around her in reciprocation and she knew that more than just their bodies was touching. They walked on against the breeze and shielded one another until they came to a high embankment next to the stream.

The water was gurgling with cheerful merriment, a bright accompaniment for both their spirits. Ann looked down and saw that the exposed roots from a big tree overhead were still lashed above the water. Many times she had sat there and dreamed while her toes dangled in the water below.

"Oh, look, Nathan," she said, as she tumbled down the grassy incline. "My dream seat is still here. I could have or do anything I wanted when I sat there."

She laughed with a special crystal sound, not realizing how beguiling and carefree she suddenly looked, slipping easily into the crevice and lying back on the bank.

"Come on," she said in laughing excitement. "Come down here. Take your shoes off! It's wonderful," she said, as her already bare feet trailed in the water.

"You're kidding," he said, but her joy and abandon was infectious and within seconds he was next to her, relaxing and laughing with her.

With the cows no longer there to keep the brush down the grove was completely overgrown and they were immersed in a heavy woodsy scent. Ann fit snugly into Nathan's arm again, as he pulled her close in the natural sanctuary of the nook. Although the sky still swirled in the distance, indicating that the threat of a storm was still near, they were surrounded by an incredible calm.

Ann looked up through the trees and remembered the hundreds of times she had sat here, the countless times she had wished for a moment exactly like this one—when she had fantasized thinking of sharing this spot in the arms of a man who loved her. She snuggled closer to Nathan and felt him respond in a soft, gentle way.

"This is nice," he said. "It's been a long time since I've felt so . . . so peaceful."

Ann remained silent and listened as the sounds of the creatures and insects made a sweet cacophony around them. The sun began to pour through, hot and insistent, as morning moved on its way. She adjusted her position. In her momentary flailing about, her fingers gently grazed his face. She looked up and saw him looking down on her with real tenderness. Her heart nearly stopped as the warmth of her response overwhelmed her. She was a well of sweetness—slow, languid, peaceful, yearning sweetness, asking only for comfort and solace, a moment at a time.

"Touching is a wonderful thing," she said softly, as she traced his lips lightly with her fingers. "Sometimes you have to touch someone before you can really know them."

He reached out and gently pushed her hair away, a special look of entreaty on his face. Ann didn't know what was really happening. She only knew that something within her was merging with him in a way that told her to speak softly and go softly until she had reached the very depths of his soul. It was there. The avenue was there and she could almost see the way.

Slowly they began to explore gently, traveling over the planes of one another's face, tracing the arms, touching the muscles in sweet stroking movements until at last their lips came together in a light, ethereal caress, so feathery that only the communion of their eyes told them it had happened.

She traced his ears and poured out all of her sweetest emotions as her fingers relayed her feelings. She began to unbutton his shirt, wanting to touch him everywhere. She felt the resilience of his hair and laid her cheek against the soft down on his chest as her lips began a slow track up his shoulder.

"Oh, Nathan," she said, "hold me. Nothing more than

86

that. . . . Just let me feel safe and warm. Show me what it means to care, really care. I've never known, but you have."

She could feel tears moistening her eyes.

Slowly he lifted her face and gently kissed the tears away. She looked at him through a mist and realized that something inside of her was always going to hurt, but this man could make it go away. She felt a grief and a longing and a yearning all at the same time and realized suddenly it wasn't Jeff that was making her hurt. It was the longing and need for him, Nathan, and the love he couldn't give her.

"I don't have to teach you anything," he whispered. "You're making me feel and touch . . . Almost as if . . . Oh, God!" he sighed in despair. "If only I could really touch and feel again. To just once be really satisfied."

His arms went around Ann and pulled her close as his lips devoured hers. "Be with me," he whispered. "You feel so warm and you smell so sweet," he said as he nuzzled her hair.

His lips began a sweet track of fire over her face until his caresses became a sweet savagery. Ann responded willingly and in the depths of her understanding she realized if she were ever to reach him she had to give him this ultimate gift. In the depths of her soul she realized she wanted to give it. Although it was a response to an agonized cry, kindness and decency dictated a reply and the yearnings of her body transformed it.

Slowly they began a gentle, poignant enactment of love as his lips trailed over her and expressed sweet, urgent endearments. "Love me," he said, "love me. I need you . . ."

She slipped from her blouse and pulled him close as the

87

soft patter of rain began to spatter over them gently. He gathered her to him and moved her into the sanctuary of an overgrown area which provided them with a natural shelter.

Slowly his strong fingers began a tender massage of her warm breasts. Her thrusting nipples responded to his touch. Gently she traced the planes of his face and pulled him closer. His caresses were urgent, as his lips devoured her breasts and his hands moved ever lower in marauding wonder. As they moved over her body and began to tug at her jeans, he lay next to her, the warmth of his body enshrouding hers. The pulse of their needs drove them on. He kissed her again and again, challenging her tongue and titillating her senses until chills of desire drove her wild. He pulled her closer, offering her every opportunity to explore him sensuously.

She responded with an invitation of her own, relaxing into total vulnerability, wanting now to share with him on any basis whatever love he had to give. She needed it as much as he. She was breathless as the moment drew near and she reveled in every exciting touch that brought her ever nearer to him.

Then suddenly, unaccountably his movements slowed and she felt a tension that hadn't been there before. He sat up in a swift movement and turned away.

"It can't happen this way. . . . Somehow it's just not right this time."

She saw the muscles tense in his back as she looked up in bewilderment. His shoulders were slumped and friction was everywhere almost as if they were in a battle of magnetic currents.

It took only seconds to understand and then her heart went out to him completely. In an instant insight she, too, realized that this way was wrong, but her yearning and need for him had not changed.

"Nathan," she said softly, "there are all kinds of ways to love. Each one right in its own way and right now I really just need you to hold me and touch me. I'm scared and lonely and I think you're the only person who can understand that."

She saw a shudder go through his body as his pride warred with his soul. Slowly he turned back to her. His eyes were troubled and angry, but slowly they softened as he struggled. Gradually he opened his arms to her. She reached out and gently touched his fingertips, never taking her eyes from his. Their hands caught in a clasp and he pulled her close. They sat in a warm embrace while the storm blew away as quickly as it had come.

After a while Nathan gently pulled her shirt over her head and straightened his own clothes. They didn't speak as he arose and pulled her to her feet next to him.

The breeze was balmy and warm as they walked back across the field. As the silence grew longer between them Ann could feel a rigid tension invading his body again and she knew he was deeply troubled. In desperation she tried to think of something else that would help, but she was at a loss.

She felt like putting her arms around him and hugging him again, but for some reason she was afraid to do it now. It was almost as if second by second she could feel him shutting her out. As they walked on toward the barns an outsider might have thought they were mere acquaintances passing the time of day. When he finally left a few moments later, although he acquiesced and touched her face gently, his eyes were troubled and she was left with an infuriating sense of frustration.

CHAPTER SEVEN

Over the next few days Ann reveled in the memory of those wonderful touching moments with Nathan, but she was also deeply troubled over his exit. To add to her uneasiness, Christopher had begun to stop by occasionally since her talk with Dale Spencer. He often had his guitar with him and they had had several discussions. She was even more impressed now by his maturity and devotion to his music. She openly encouraged him, but the thought of Nathan's resistance still made her very uncomfortable. The feeling was aggravated by the seemingly unending complexity of her own relationship with him.

The weather had warmed up considerably and she was enjoying a Saturday afternoon at her new home site. Randolph had just left, after carefully explaining how inverted swimming pool construction was going to be used to form the half-circle frames that would support the earth covering her house. He must have passed Nathan as Nathan gunned his truck into the lane.

Ann was walking around visualizing the placement of her window wall, the greenhouse with Jacuzzi pool, and the huge heat-pack fireplace, all of which would work together with a windmill to provide the energy for her home. The moment the truck screeched to a halt Ann knew something terrible was about to happen.

Nathan advanced, a stormcloud of emotion as his stern features were fixed in an outraged grimace. Ann remembered the tender gentleness of his face just a few days before. She recoiled as this angry man stomped towards her.

"I've just been talking with Christopher," he said, looking around the messy beginning construction with disdain. "Haven't you got anything better to do with yourself than to interfere in other people's affairs?"

Ann was appalled by the brutality of his attack. There was no earthly reason for such emotion. He was almost like a man driven by demonic forces. Her heart was racing as she delved deeply for the strength and control to handle this situation properly. She willed herself to calm down as she smiled brightly.

"I'm sorry," she said, not quite able to avoid a little shakiness in her voice. "I don't understand what you're talking about . . ."

"Don't understand, hell!" he shouted. "What do you mean by encouraging Christopher to participate in that stupid music contest? Don't I have enough trouble with that interfering teacher, Spencer?"

"Well," she said, determined not to let him ruffle her, "it seems like a good idea in view of Christopher's talent and dedication. Really, though, I didn't have a thing to do with this. . . . Christopher had made his decision about this long before he discussed it with me. I don't know why you're so upset. It's not interfering with any of his work or studies, is it?"

Her unflappable calm had an immediate effect on him. She could actually see his anger subsiding.

91

"Well, no," he said, looking to the ground, "but it's just that I don't want him to get any crazy ideas. Our family has worked too long and hard for what we have and Christopher has a certain responsibility . . ."

"I'm sure Christopher understands that," she said. "He seems like a really sensible young man."

He looked at her ready with another retort, but it apparently died on his lips as he turned away, pushed his cap back over his unruly hair, and shook his head. He planted his heavy work shoes in the soft mud and glared at her as he looped his fingers through the belt on his faded jeans.

"Well, maybe you're right," he said in disgust. "He plays with that damned guitar all of the time, anyway. He's bound to get tired of any real studying. I guess the worst thing I could do is make a big fuss over it."

Ann was impressed as she watched this visible exercise in controlled deduction. In a way this was almost too easy. She was left with a feeling of disquiet. As if in response to her troubled thoughts, his expression softened. He dropped the subject of his anger completely and Ann had a premonition that Christopher really wasn't what was bothering him at all.

"Quite a project you've got going here," he said conversationally.

"Yes," she said, following his cue uneasily. "We're just beginning." She pointed toward a pile of construction materials. "Here, let me show you the plans . . ." She began unrolling the voluminous number of sketches and maneuvered so he could look. She was scolded by a noisy cardinal, who voiced his displeasure over the intrusion into his domain. They both laughed and with this diversion the stifling uneasiness seemed to abate.

Ann's relief was enormous.

"In a way," she said gaily, "I'm like a bird. I want a natural place where I can eat, and bathe . . . and . . ." she shrugged her shoulders theatrically and rolled her eyes skyward, "hide away."

She laughed.

One of the birds flew away with a straw.

"Even to nest and court in," she said, suddenly coy as she looked into his eyes.

Nathan's face clouded. He was obviously not impressed with her attempt at clever metaphor. In sudden comprehension, Ann saw to the heart of the conflict and realized she had just unintentionally sparked the memory of his failure in the woods.

His eyes narrowed.

"Looks to me like you're planning nothing more than a glorified cave."

There was a taunting note in his voice, his easy, casual tone growing perceptibly sharper.

"As I recall, women who lived in caves were just grabbed by the hair and dragged off. That was their way of courting. Didn't need anything else!"

As he spoke his hand reached out and grasped the back of her startled head. He pulled her roughly to him as his lips came crushing down on hers savagely, sending her into an immediate dizzying response, but she quickly rallied. This was not an act of intimacy. It was an act of rage and she was honestly insulted.

"Stop it!" she demanded, as she pulled herself roughly away. "You know, you can go just a little too far with this macho act of yours, Nathan Warner! Just once," she said, her eyes darting between flushed cheeks as she searched for the most spiteful words she could think of, "I wish the real Nathan Warner would speak and when he does I wish he would speak to me—not someone else!"

Her entire body was heaving with scalding, repressed fury as she twisted away in disgust.

Again there was an almost instantaneous transformation as Nathan changed before her eyes, but not before she saw the piercing wound her barbed retort had inflicted. Pain shot through his entire countenance. He looked at the ground, clenched his fists, and turned guiltily away.

Concern quickly replaced her indignation as she watched him walk silently away. As his truck spun off she saw his angry hurt eyes. She had been cruel and she was suddenly ashamed of her lack of sensitivity, but, *surely,* she thought as she rallied to her own defense, *I have a right to defend myself. He may have problems, but that doesn't give him the right to be abusive, either. . . .*

She stood for a moment in indignant reflection and then her entire countenance sagged. *Damn,* she thought. *The other day I thought maybe we were going to find a way to get along. . . .*

She went back to watching the noisy cardinals. Their chatter was a nasty reminder of her own emotions. She wished now she had called out to him. She wished she had forced him to talk. . . . And then anger washed over her again. To hell with him. He was out of line. Only an idiot would take that.

When she returned to her parents' home a little later she had finally calmed down and come to an impasse with her warring emotions, but she was still deeply troubled. As she went into the living room she saw the trunk she had taken from Nathan's attic.

Almost as if drawn to it magnetically, she went to it and gingerly opened its ornate lid. The chest itself was a work of art, richly carved with flowers and obviously lovingly created by someone who cared deeply. Slowly she began to sift through the contents. She had an uncanny feeling of intrusion as the intimate personal items of a couple, deeply in love more than a hundred years before, began to emerge. There were items of clothing and a few utilitarian gadgets, but for the most part it was obvious that the trunk contained highly personal, intimate keepsakes that had value only to those who had shared them. There was a picture of a young, plain-looking couple, but even the rigid confines of early photography could not hide their radiance as they looked at one another. The Bible was well worn and marked. It fell open to the Song of Solomon and also to the other great love stories as the pages continued to fall open on much-used passages. The Book of Ruth had been read often and as Ann glanced at the opening passages she could see how this young wife must have identified with the "wither thou goest" she had marked plainly.

She could feel a certain warm charisma emanating from the trunk. A great and deep love had been shared by its owners as they had shared hardships and adversities and those vibrations were still very much alive. Beneath the Bible there was a stack of letters tied with a ribbon grown yellow with age. Ann knew they were private, yet something drew her to extract one from the pile. As she opened it a heavy perfume strengthened by the mustiness of age assailed her senses, but the clarity and sincerity of the passages, despite the stilted form of Victorian prose, moved her deeply. This was a young woman writing to her husband of only a few months during their first separation.

As Ann read through the mundane chitchat of everyday things she also noted a sense of care and sharing fortified

by an absolute faith in their destiny, which was beautiful
—too beautiful to really exist and yet, as Ann felt tears
around the edges of her eyes, she knew that, although it
might border more on fairy tale than reality, that's what
she wanted, too. That's the kind of life and love she wanted to have and to share.

She needed someone who had it together, who could
meet her one on one and give her the strength and support
she needed. What she didn't need was problems—serious
emotional problems. What she didn't need was Nathan
Warner, and the events of this afternoon were more than
enough to convince her of that on a rational basis. Though
as far as her emotions and her physical response to him
were concerned she needed more work.

As she cemented these thoughts firmly into her mind,
she picked up the vase again. She ran her fingers over it
gently. It really was exquisite. She remembered that she
had mentioned it to Randolph and learned that he was
something of an art buff. He had mentioned several places
where she might learn a little more about it. She'd written
them down, but now, as if in resolution of her thoughts
just moments before, she decided to give him a call. What
she needed was a diversion—a serious diversion.

She reached for the phone in the kitchen and began to
dial before she remembered in chagrin that they were on
a party line. She heard a loud squawk from a woman she
recognized as Anna Belle Cooper, long known for her
scandalous and lengthy dissertations on the telephone.

"You know that Taylor girl has finally come home,"
Ann heard. Normally Ann would not have listened, but
she found herself glued to the receiver, as she let out a soft
little gasp. "You know she always was pretty loose, but
now she's come back all high and mighty, runnin' three

or four men, and she's building that outlandish house . . . You know, I don't know what we're coming to around here . . ."

The woman's voice faded away as Ann finally forced herself to hang up the receiver. She was filled with an indignant rage just as her father came through the door.

"What's the matter, daughter?"

"Oh," she said in exasperation, "I was just going to make a call and that old biddy, Mrs. Cooper, was on the line talking about me!"

"Ah, hell, young'n, nobody pays any attention to that old windbag."

He laughed and gave her chin a little nudge.

"Well, I don't know," she said. "It seems like every time I turn around someone is making a snide remark."

"Now what do you mean by that?" he asked. He was all fatherly concern.

"Well, take Nathan Warner, for instance. I've gone out of my way to be nice to him, you know, the way Mr. Shuman asked me to, and yet . . ."

She could feel herself growing scarlet as intimate moments flashed dizzyingly through her head.

"Yes," her father said, waiting patiently for her to finish.

"Well, I encouraged Christopher to pursue his musical interests and Nathan just got so snippy. . . . You know, I could really like him, but he just seems so moody and difficult . . ."

She looked at her father and realized she really had never intended to discuss anything so personal with him, yet it gave her such a relief. His understanding was like a precious gift she had never known was there.

"Aye, that he is, honey. He's a man who has had some

real problems and I know . . . maybe I shouldn't say anything. You're certainly old enough to take care of yourself, but you know he's kind of gotten a reputation as a womanizer since his wife's death. A real love 'em and leave 'em kind of guy, so you might be wanting to look over the field a little."

"Oh, Dad," she said as she smiled shyly. "I'm not talking about anything serious. It's just been one of those days."

"Now don't get me wrong," her father said astutely, tipping her chin up and meeting her gaze squarely. "Nathan's a good man. He'd make a wonderful husband for a woman who knew how to handle him."

"Now, Dad," she said, honestly exasperated.

He smiled.

"As a matter of fact," she said, "I was just going to call Randolph. You know he's a lot of fun to be with."

"He's that architect fella?"

"Yes," said Ann. "You've got to come down and see. We're going to pour the foundation and frames next week, but right now I'm going to see if he can help me find out something about this vase we found in Tanya's attic."

She was walking towards the living room to show it to him.

"You mean Nathan's attic, don't you? Not saying his name won't make him go away." There was a droll musing look on his face that she decided to ignore.

She went back to the phone and within moments she had a date with Randolph for that evening. She looked at her watch and realized she'd better get cracking.

As Nathan's outrageous conduct again came to mind, she really wondered what had gotten into him. He had been undeniably abusive. She had gone out of her way, admittedly, to try and be cute, but a simple little metaphor over the habits of birds shouldn't have ticked him off like that. Really there was no excuse. She was through making excuses for both him and herself. Enough was definitely enough, but still she had this sad little feeling, a feeling of remorse that came from deep within.

If only, she thought.

Damn if only!

She was really angry. She finally acknowledged it. Deeply and furiously angry.

But for the moment, she thought, as she forced herself to calm down, *Randolph was dashing, handsome, and witty.* She was going to look smashing for him tonight. It was definitely time for a new interest.

She dressed carefully, having decided to use the silky culottes she had discarded when she dressed for the dance several weeks before. She thought again of her breathless anticipation that night and was clearly displeased with her sophomoric reactions of the past weeks.

As she gave herself a spray of her favorite light cologne and fluffed her hair one last time, she heard Randolph's car coming up the drive. When she greeted him moments later she was sparkling.

"Well, aren't you the lovely one tonight," he said as he came in. He went on to greet her parents in an easy way and both warmed to him.

"Well, have you decided where we are going on our first bona fide date?" he teased. "This is the first time we'll be together without the pretense of talking about the house."

"Very funny," said Ann. "Actually, since you're being so cute, I do have something else I want to talk to you about."

She took his arm and moved him towards the chest. She opened it and handed him the vase.

"Lovely," he said. "This looks like something really fine. Is this the vase you were telling me about?"

"Yes," said Ann.

"Well, I'll tell you what," he said with a roguish smile. "It just so happens that there is an exhibit of Oriental art at Ohio State University right now. It's open tonight. What do you say we have a look and see what we can find out?"

"Sounds great." She smiled.

"Shall we, then? I'm sure we can find a cozy spot for dinner afterward. Don't wait up for us," he called as they said their farewell to her parents.

They both laughed and Ann was pleased that her parents seemed to like him so much. As she looked into his smiling eyes she really did feel warm and happy with him. While he designed her home it was almost as if he had a second sense when it came to her desires. Again a momentary thought of Nathan flashed through her mind, but it quickly receded when she felt the strength of his hands as he handed her into his zippy sports car.

"Shall we leave the top down?" he inquired.

"Yes, please," said Ann.

It was a lovely evening and the wind blowing over her would be wonderfully exhilarating. She laughed as they drove down the lane. She knew she was going to have a wonderful time.

It was wonderful. They laughed and joked until finally Ann was sure she could laugh no more only to go off on yet another cascade of giggles.

The exhibit was fantastic. With Randolph there as her expert guide and the beautifully published handbook he gallantly bought for her, she was quickly transported into the marvelous, ethereal world of Oriental art. Before the evening was over they had discussed the vase with the curator of the exhibit. He advised them to have it appraised by an auction firm specializing in items of that kind.

Laden with names, addresses, and phone numbers they went on to dinner at the exciting Jai Alai nightclub and ended up dancing until the wee hours of the morning.

As they drove up the lane of the Taylor homestead, Ann yawned luxuriously. "Too bad you still have such a long drive to Zanesville," she said.

"Yes, it is," he said, a bit drolly. "But then I'm sure Mother Taylor wouldn't relish the thought of my staying over."

Ann looked at him sharply for just a moment, but then she saw insidious teasing in his eyes and knew he was not, in any way, serious.

"No, I don't think so," she laughed.

"Ah, well, then we really must get on with the house!"

"You cad," she said as she felt laughter overtaking her again. She couldn't remember when she had laughed so much. Really not since . . .

She flinched as she thought of Jeff.

"Oh," he said as he watched her change in humor. "Why the sad face? Have I said something wrong?"

"Oh, no," she said. "It's just that at times you remind me of someone. Someone I once had very good times with."

She smiled as she reached out to touch his cheek.

"You're really very sweet and I'm glad you're building my house."

"The pleasure's all mine," he said, pulling her closer. "You're really a wonderful woman."

He kissed her very gently and Ann felt herself responding to him warmly. It was a very comforting embrace—one that she knew could create real contentment.

She pulled away at last and looked into his eyes. The wind ruffled his hair and created a certain flair and dash about him that was very attractive. He kissed her again, this time more deeply, and Ann found herself responding more ardently. It was nice and made her feel very good, but more important, in full control of herself.

Yes, she thought as they broke apart and Randolph walked her up to the door. *She had been right. Randolph was the kind of man she needed. Not someone who could shatter her into a million pieces every time she turned around. Not someone like Nathan Warner!*

She gave him a last kiss good-bye and waved him off as his little car zoomed away. She felt good. Very good. It was nice to know that she was capable of finally getting her life in order.

Over the next few days, as the construction of her house began in earnest, she found that she was coming to rely very much on the warm intimate rapport she was building with Randolph. He just seemed to grow on her. The petting and caressing of their lovemaking and casual caresses was very satisfying, but she felt no urge to give herself over to him in wild abandon.

Not like, she thought, *that shameless scene she had had with Nathan in the barn.*

She flushed with shame as she thought of it and yet something turned in her and made her trace the track of his lips whenever she thought of him. It was only her continued, very deep anger that kept her from full acknowledgment of her real feelings.

She really hated him when she thought of his disgusting "caveman antics," as she now referred to them. He had really been utterly debased in venting his anger in such a crude way.

She had opened her soul to him, offered him the nectar of her existence, and he had repaid her with brutal insult. She had endured, excused, and even shouldered the blame for some of his antics, but this last encounter had marked the end for her.

CHAPTER EIGHT

Before Ann knew it the full force of summer and its flurry of activities was upon her. She had taken the treasures from Nathan's house and worked diligently on the Lost Arts Festival project with Tanya, although Tanya was still somewhat distant with her. Christopher was ecstatic over his music project and the prospect of the county and state fairs created their own special pressures.

Ann realized that she had not actually seen or spoken to Nathan in some time other than a wave or two. After that last unsettling confrontation she had retained such a sense of bitterness that she truthfully had no desire to address him. She knew her mood was not conducive to anything of a positive nature. He, for the most part, along with all of the other farmers in the area, was pressed for time as he finished planting and then went on to the hectic duties of baling hay, followed closely by the harvesting of wheat and rye and baling of straw.

Then too, Ann was so involved with the construction of her house that she really could not account for the passage of time. In the meantime her feelings of hostility towards Nathan began to abate somewhat as she became more and more involved with Randolph. Whereas Nathan left her with a sense of frustration that she really did not enjoy,

Randolph was an absolute joy. His companionship was growing increasingly important to her.

She had practically forgotten about the vase until a letter arrived from the auction firm where she had made an inquiry. They needed to see the vase to make an honest appraisal. Ann realized she was going to need to discuss this with Nathan or else just forget about it. In examining the vase again she instinctively felt it was a real treasure and really should not be hidden away. She had been told ball-park figures in excess of five hundred thousand dollars were not unheard of if the vase was an authentic specimen. Then, too, she thought of Christopher as he performed so eloquently the night of the dance and of Tanya with her feisty determination to become a farmer, not to mention the joy Grandpa Warner would feel should it be truly valuable.

She squared her shoulders and set her jaw firmly. She had come this far. There was no reason to drop it now. She didn't really relish seeing Nathan again, and yet her heart seemed to pick up a special staccato beat at the very thought of it. *You're a fool,* she said to herself, but nevertheless she was momentarily breathless as she placed the vase carefully into the trunk again.

Ann knew that Christopher had a birthday coming up within the next week. She impulsively purchased a book about the lives of great composers and decided she would combine the giving of this gift with the discussion of the vase.

She timed her visit to coincide with the evening chores and was gratified to find Christopher in the kitchen, again preparing dinner. He was overjoyed with her visit and when she presented him with the book insisted that she sit down and listen to his first serious composition. He was preparing it for the competition.

"Here," he said excitedly. "Let me get you some fruit and cheese. We've even got some wine."

"No, really, that's not necessary," she said, laughing.

He was as excited as a flustered busybody.

"Oh, come on," he said. "That's the way big city folks get in the mood for things like this, from what I hear. And . . . the song is . . . Well, it's a love song."

He said the last words in a rush trying to make them sound like an offhand comment of no real importance, but Ann looked at him and realized he really was very excited and her reaction was terribly important to him.

"Well, all right," she said, "but *you* aren't going to have any wine, are you?"

"No," he said, quickly arranging apples, cheese, and wine in front of her attractively. "I'm going to play."

Again the guitar became a symphony in his hands as he staged himself across the room from her. He had created a wonderful mournful melody, heightened by the intricacy of runs and strums that created an insistent beat. He kept his eyes glued to his music, which he had painstakingly committed to paper. When he did glance up his eyes were pools of admiration, completely in spirit with his music. As the wild crescendo slowed to a soulful ebb, he reached to the side and quickly produced a clarinet. Ann gasped in surprise. She had no idea that Christopher played other instruments as well. Soon the clarinet wailed forth in sweet melodic tones and Ann knew her instincts had been very right. Christopher had a true calling. Music was his life. If only somehow they could get Nathan to see it.

Almost as if an apparition on call to her subconscious, Nathan suddenly appeared. He was in his usual rugged clothes. His snug jeans and damp shirt clung faithfully to his lean muscular form and he was covered with an extra layer of dust from baling straw.

"Christopher, what's going on here? I thought you were getting supper for the rest of us while we finished up the chores. You know we have to get back to the fields tonight."

His eyes were stormy with irritation as they raked over Ann.

"I am," said Christopher a little sheepishly. "It's just that, well. . . . Today is my birthday and Ann brought me a gift. While the chicken was finishing up I was just letting her hear the song I composed."

At the mention of birthday, Nathan looked thoroughly chagrined. "I'm sorry, Chris . . . I guess I forgot." He rubbed the back of his head with a grimace. "Listen, go on . . . Take your things and go on and practice. I'll finish up supper."

Ann had watched this scene unfold with keen interest. Again she was astounded by the obvious complexities of this family, as Christopher beamed a big smile to his dad and quickly went out beneath a big tree to continue with his music.

Ann smiled, very pleased. She was happy to see that Nathan was showing some indication of being capable of reason, inspired, no doubt, by a sincere affection for his son.

"What are you smiling about?" he scowled. "Didn't you understand what I said the last time we spoke?"

His eyes lit on the tray Christopher had prepared.

She was instantly angry, but she decided to ignore his ugly address and handle this in her own way.

"Not at all," she said coolly. "Actually I came over to discuss the vase I found in your attic."

She picked up an apple.

Slowly his eyes watched as her lips nibbled the fruit and savored the sweet juices that spurted from the first crisp bite. Ann could feel herself responding as his eyes roamed over her face and then dropped slowly, coming to rest on her cleavage, which came to a neat V in her tailored white blouse.

She could feel her emotions warring again.

"Would you like some cheese?" she asked, meeting his eyes in an unspoken challenge. "Or perhaps some wine? The Greeks and Romans, you know, thought of the combination as a special ambrosia, straight from the gods."

"I wouldn't know about such things," he said in his slow drawling voice. "I'm just a simple man of simple pleasures. I leave those sophisticated ideas to those who think they're important."

His eyes continued to look her over and Ann could feel herself growing warm with acute irritation as the examination began to assume the overtones of a practiced appraisal, usually used in looking over stock. She remembered then their last ugly scene together and she recalled Mrs. Cooper's comments in her telephone discussion of Ann's alleged "free and easy" behavior. She suddenly heard herself speaking in an abrupt, unthinking way.

"I don't know what makes you think you have the right to treat me the way you do."

She gave him a calculating look.

"You know, my dad says you're quite a womanizer, in your own right, when you want to be—a regular love 'em and leave 'em cad."

She met his eyes in a direct confrontation.

He looked away, thoroughly affronted. His perusal of Ann had actually been an unconscious gesture of which he was not really aware.

"Maybe he's trying to protect me. He thinks I'm attracted to you." She looked away, somewhat flushed. "In a way, of course, I am."

She gazed at him, openly amused at the discomfort her impetuous brazenness had caused him. He wasn't the only one who could be outrageous. It felt good to turn the tables on him for once.

"Those are the things," she went on, "that women savor and use in their private fantasies."

She spoke smugly in a low soft voice and lowered her eyes discreetly.

"Of course, they're meaningless, situations we'd never want in real life."

Nathan continued to look at her, confounded by her erratic behavior.

Then she lifted her head and defiantly met his gaze again.

"Surely you have your fantasies, too," she continued, determined to press the point.

Pain rippled slowly over his face and settled in a granite grimace as his eyes came to rest on the photo sitting on the mantle across the room. Ann followed his movements and saw him visibly concede as he searched the face of his wife smiling so prettily from the picture.

"Oh, Nathan," she said, suddenly contrite. "I'm sorry! Why are we doing this? Why must we hurt each other?"

"Dad," said Tanya as she entered the room. "Is supper ready?"

She stopped when she saw Ann and was immediately wary.

"Yeah, sure, sugar," said Nathan a little sheepishly. "Ann just came over to talk to us about that vase the two of you found in the attic."

Sensing that Tanya was a little uncomfortable, Ann tried to put the best face on the occasion. "And to see you, too," she said brightly. "You know the Lost Arts Festival is only a few weeks away."

Tanya flinched openly at the mention of the festival, but before Ann could examine this puzzling reaction Christopher also bounced into the room, his spirit ever indomitable.

"And don't forget that she remembered my birthday," he said.

"Well, I didn't forget your birthday," said Grandpa Warner as he too came in, his arms laden with a huge bakery box.

A sigh escaped from Nathan and he visibly relaxed. His fist unclenched and a solid grimace of relief spread over his face. He massaged his dark, unruly hair as his eyes met Ann's. She fully comprehended for the first time his daily struggle to meet all of the needs of his family. Again she felt an irrepressible yearning. She wished she could go to him and help him. He needed her help, but she knew the time wasn't right. And it might not ever be.

Actually it seemed with each passing day they grew further apart and she really despaired of ever meeting him again as they had on that fateful day in the woods. She looked at him again and searched his face, something she was beginning to do habitually.

His eyes met hers in speculation. She watched as he seemed to struggle with himself.

110

"You said you wanted to talk about something?"

"Yes," she said hesitantly.

She was honestly puzzled and didn't know what to expect next. She felt his eyes boring into her as the silence grew taut.

Christopher and Grandpa Warner were busy in the kitchen and their lively chatter was a portentous foil as the tension grew. Tanya watched them both warily. Nathan looked toward the kitchen and then met Ann's eyes again.

"Let's take a walk," he said softly, "and talk about it. Supper's not quite ready yet."

Ann heard Tanya gasp as she turned and left the room wordlessly, but Ann saw only Nathan as she felt her spirit reach out to touch his again.

"Sure," she said.

They walked down through the yard and strolled around the century-old complex. She could feel the physical magnetism of his body. In spite of the straw chaff and the aroma of machinery, gasoline, and oil, he was attractive in a disturbingly animal way. Ann knew he was searching for words. Feeling much the same herself, she remained silent until at last he spoke.

"That was kind of a low blow I gave back there—I mean coming on so strong about Christopher again."

"Well, I guess I was in there swinging, too," she said in relief. "It's just that I've really been upset over the way we ended up in our last meeting—you know, over at the house," she said hurriedly.

"I know," he said.

He looked at the ground sheepishly as he plunged his hands into the pockets of his jeans and then searched through the pockets of his Western-cut shirt for something he never found.

"I guess I just can't keep from making an ass out of myself when I'm around you . . . Look," he said as he stopped and turned her toward him. "I really like you. I want . . . Well, I don't know what I want."

He massaged his neck and looked at her wearily.

"Can't we just start all over again?" he said in exasperation. "At least be decent to each other. Friends?"

Ann's heart was racing as she looked into his eyes. She would never have dreamed he was capable of such sensitivity. She knew in that moment that she loved him and wanted him more than anything in the world and because of that love, she'd take whatever he had to give.

"I don't see why not," she said softly. "I'm tired of fighting, too."

"Hey, I'll tell you what!" he said in sudden exuberance. "You're looking for things for the Lost Arts Festival. Let me take you for a drive over in the Amish country this Sunday. You know there's a settlement around Plainsville."

"I'd love it," she said. "Bring Tanya and Christopher, too!"

Her eyes were sparkling and she had to muster her inner resources to keep tears from flowing.

"Now I have to talk to you about this vase," she said.

"Oh, the hell with the vase," he said boisterously. "Do whatever you want to with it."

"But, Nathan," she said in exasperation, "it could really be very valuable. This is important."

"Okay," he said.

She knew he really wasn't very impressed.

"Go on and handle it," he said. "I guess that's better than leaving it in the attic."

"You don't mind if I have it appraised then?"

"No, not at all," he said, laughing. "Now let's go in and have some birthday cake with Christopher. That boy is mighty partial to you."

"He *is* pretty good, isn't he?" Nathan said quietly.

Ann looked at Nathan, a puzzled expression on her face. She had been gazing out the window almost daydreaming as the car raced along the straight asphalt.

"Christopher, I mean."

"Well, yes, I guess so. What exactly are you talking about?" she asked curiously.

"You know . . . His music."

The flat fields whizzed by, providing a fitting scenario for her startled thoughts. She groped for appropriate words. Nathan looked straight ahead as though he were doing no more than passing the time of day with her.

"Yes, of course he is," she said finally, "but what's—"

"Well, I guess I've just been thinking, and . . . Maybe I'm being a little muleheaded. . . ."

"Why, Nathan! That's wonderful—not that you're muleheaded," she said laughing, "but that . . ."

She smiled.

"Oh, anyway, Christopher is going to be so happy!"

"Now just a minute. I'm not going overboard on this. I still think Christopher has certain responsibilities—"

"Oh, I know," said Ann, "but just the fact that you're willing to go maybe halfway."

The day had already been wonderful. Nathan had arrived around ten saying that everyone else was busy so it looked as though they were on their own. They had driven out in the warm sunshine and within an hour began to approach the Amish settlement, as they met carriage after somber carriage of these God-fearing farmers who lived exactly as their forefathers had one hundred years ago. They were returning home from church.

Their horses made a funny clop-clop sound on the modern pavement, creating a paradox which was almost uncanny. Everything about them exuded a rigid nineteenth-century independence, but their modern industriousness was more than evident as Ann and Nathan passed large handsome farms at lengthy intervals along the road.

They seemed to bask in each other's company as they joked and passed idle chitchat. With Nathan's mention of Christopher's responsibilities Tanya came to Ann's mind. She thought of Tanya's desires and realized this might be the perfect opportunity to mention this to Nathan.

"You know," she began hesitantly, "Tanya has some very admirable ambitions, too."

Nathan looked at her and she sensed a bit of sharpness. It really was a little presumptuous of her to offer him advice, but at the same time it also seemed right.

"Oh, you mean all of that talk about her taking over the farm. That's just talk. You know she won't end up thinking about anything else except boys and babies and things . . ."

"Nathan Warner!" she said in total exasperation. "Where have you been during the past decade?"

He looked at her with a startled expression, but she also saw his jaw clench ever so slightly.

Oh boy, she thought to herself, *here goes another beautiful day. . . .*

She took a deep breath.

"You really should give her and yourself more credit for intelligence—"

She stopped as she looked around in sudden confusion.

Nathan was turning into a long drive, and instead of answering her he was waving to the family driving ahead of them in a carriage as he passed them carefully.

"Where are we going?" she asked.

"Well, you wanted to find things for your project, didn't you. I'm going to introduce you to Jonathan Harmon and his family—friends of mine."

"You're kidding," she said. "That's wonderful! You know, you never cease to amaze me."

"I'll bet," he said.

There was a mischievous smile playing about his face and the tension that had whispered about them just seconds before dissipated completely.

They pulled into the drive next to the house and waited patiently for the carriage to arrive. As they did so, Ann couldn't help but make a quick comparison to Nathan's farmyard. What was missing here, though, in a funny way, was life. The verve and hope of the future. The adherence to total lack of color or any indication of frivolity left a dark impression.

She shivered, but then immediately chastised herself as Jonathan Harmon came up and greeted Nathan in a warm and robust way.

"Nathan, how nice to see you on the day of our Lord."

He was followed by his wife and daughter. His son gave a friendly wave and went on toward the barn to take care of the horse and carriage.

"Jonathan, this is my friend, Miss Ann Taylor."

Jonathan scratched the full beard that marked him as a married man and nodded to Nathan in satisfied approval.

"Jonathan has been a good friend to me over the past few years. We've both learned a lot from each other."

The men's eyes met in mutual agreement.

"You're standing on one of the most productive, efficient farms in the country," said Nathan. "Not a thing is wasted and everything is controlled naturally."

As they went on into the house Ann was soon immersed in a funny, austere mixture of an antiquated life-style with just a touch here and there of the twentieth century. There was a small generator for some electrical needs on the farm, but in the house the smells of kerosene lamps and wood stoves mingled with the undeniably delicious aroma of a traditional Sunday dinner.

As Jonathan's wife and daughter scurried around in their long black dresses, Ann was inexplicably caught up in a kind of bankrupt nostalgia. She was fascinated with this glimpse of the past, but she also immediately missed modern conveniences she had long taken for granted.

Mrs. Harmon and her daughter were rosy and friendly, but it was obvious that they were submissive to the men in the family. They all enjoyed wonderful wholesome food, followed by incredibly rich pastries, including old-fashioned peach pie. After the dinner Ann intuitively understood that she was to remain with the women while Nathan went out on the porch with Jonathan and his son. It was obvious that the family was going to honor the rule about rest on the Sabbath as they remained in their Sunday finery and welcomed the entertaining of guests.

Alone the women became talkative and chatty. When Ann told them about her Lost Arts project they became very excited and soon Ann had a treasure of items and folklore. Outside she heard wisps of Nathan's conversation and heard him talking of crops and farming procedures. There was a sense of friendly rivalry, but she also realized Nathan was questioning very carefully. There was a friendly debate now and then and finally Nathan arose.

"Jonathan, I know you have pretty strict customs, but I wonder if you'd mind if we took Ann down and showed her around the barns and fields?"

Jonathan looked at him sagely.

"Why, whatever makes you think our women don't go around the barns?"

There was a merry twinkle in his eyes.

Soon the whole group was wandering about. As they walked over the green grass beneath giant shade trees Nathan took Ann's arm and guided her expertly about. A familiar warmth enveloped her and she realized anew how much she had come to care for this complex man.

An hour later they were on their way again. Ann was still a little astounded by the events of the day thus far. Almost as if their conversation had never been interrupted Nathan took up where they had left off just before turning into the Harmons' lane.

"Owning land and being a farmer is a tremendous responsibility—more so than it ever was before."

He looked at Ann, gauging her expression carefully.

"It takes a special strength and a man's got to feel it and believe in it and know that what he's doing with the land today could have consequences for hundreds of years."

Ann remained silent but attentive, feeling it was wise to see what he was leading up to.

"With the need for so much operating capital and the increasing use of all these chemicals and unnatural things, if the true men of the land aren't whiz-bang businessmen as well they're soon in over their heads. Before long they've got no choice but to scrap all of the soil conservation and advances in quality for intensive production that is wearing the land out, pumping our people full of carcinogens, and finally running the independent farmer out so that those big conglomerates can take over. . . ."

There was a scowl on his face.

"Why, you know I've seen them out west on vegetable farms where they plow whole fields of carrots under just because they didn't harvest them in time and now the carrots were too big for the fancy picker they run by remote control. It was called a cost-effective measure. Meanwhile, people are starving and everyone else is being robbed in the grocery store."

"Oh, but there's got to be more to it than that," said Ann.

"Oh, sure there is," he said, "but what it really comes down to is that the last stronghold of American independence and free enterprise is being destroyed through a combination of big business, government interference, and downright greed. You know, when you get right down to it, food is the number one key to basic survival. The man who controls that controls the world."

Ann was amazed. She had no idea that Nathan felt so strongly and she was impressed with the obvious depth of his reasoning.

"They've gotten so mechanized that they're even trying to turn creatures into machines. Chickens in tiny little cages stacked on each other, baby calves fed nothing but milk in dark barns, our cows and pigs and everything condemned to totally unnatural lives. I'm telling you it's a blasphemy and sooner or later we're all going to pay!"

"But, Nathan," she said. "I don't see how . . ."

"Well, I'm telling you there are better ways and the old ways weren't all bad. They're finding out now that these new so-called advances are not all that they're cracked up

118

to be and in some instances they are downright wasteful. When Mona died . . ."

He stopped.

Ann saw something flicker in his face. He looked at her and she saw incredible pain. She started to reach out, but she saw him stiffen. His hands gripped the wheel and he looked straight ahead.

"When Mona died," he went on softly.

Suddenly she saw something in his body relax.

"You know," he said, his voice barely audible, "that's the first time I've ever said that word."

"What word?" said Ann.

"Died. Dead," he said with vehemence.

Ann knew this was something very private and she remained silent.

Suddenly he looked at her, an expression of grim resolution on his face. Slowly he pursed his lips and forced his face into a harried grin. For a moment she thought the hard mantle was descending again and then he took a big breath. He looked at her and reached out to touch her arm.

"Thank you," he said softly. "I think I'm finally beginning to understand."

Ann fought tears as all of her emotions gushed forth, but she managed to give him a bright smile as her hand went over his. They remained that way for a few moments, neither speaking, and then Nathan continued resolutely.

"When Mona died . . . I was so bitter and angry knowing she might have gotten something from all of those things we were using that I just about went mad. I started going out for long drives and one day I ended up over here and just accidentally met Jonathan when I impulsively turned down his lane one day. I've learned so much from him, but at the same time realized how important it is to find the best of the new ways. I like Jonathan, but there's something about him that depresses me, too."

"There's plenty about him that depresses me," said Ann with a teasing little smile. "Seeing women so firmly in their 'place' is almost mind-boggling. I mean, I just really never understood—"

"Yeah, well, I don't see so much wrong with that," he said.

A mischievous smile played over his face again.

"Seriously, though," he went on, "it's not that I'm just bullheaded over Christopher and his music. I can see now that there is something to it, but his responsibility is to the land and the traditions of our family. It's not just some macho thing on my part. I'm not trying to pass on a knighthood or anything like that. The situation in this country is serious. The possibility of famine isn't as ridiculous as you might think in our society. Not even a percentile of a percentile of our population is capable of growing food and providing for themselves. It's gotten to the point now where there is virtually only a handful of people like me and we've got to make sure our kids carry it on . . ."

"Well, what's the matter with giving Tanya some consideration?" asked Ann. "She's not a little child. She's a young woman giving serious thought to her future and I think she knows exactly what she wants and she's very sincere."

"Now I've already told you what I think about that."

"Okay, okay, maybe you're right, but on the other hand you wouldn't deny her the right to follow in your footsteps, would you? I mean if she's really willing to try and she sticks to it?"

He looked at her with a grimace and then brought his hand to his chin in reflection.

"Well, in a way it doesn't seem right, but then . . . Well, in a way you're right. She's got the touch and the feel. I always figured she'd make a hell of a farmer's wife."

"Well, why not a hell of a farmer?" said Ann, pressing her advantage.

"Well, where would that leave Christopher, then?" he asked almost unthinkingly.

"Right where they both are, right now," she said. "There's room for both of them, isn't there? Instead of being so hyper over Christopher you ought to see that you've got double potential there. Both of those kids have got a long way to go before they make their final decisions."

"Yeah, well, what do you know," he finally said in joking capitulation.

He reached out and gave her chin a nudge.

I know, she said to herself softly, *I care about them and you very much. . . .*

"You know," he said, almost as if this were something they discussed every day, "it would seem kind of funny having two or three houses in a family."

Ann looked at him, again amazed by his startling turn of thoughts.

"What on earth are you talking about now?"

"Oh, I was just thinking," he said a little shyly, "if we can ever get our feelings sorted out . . . Well, there's sure enough houses to go around, aren't there?"

"Nathan," she said softly.

She saw him grip the wheel and look straight ahead.

"So!" he said suddenly—almost as if his thoughts had braked to a screeching halt.

He looked at her a little sheepishly. She sensed a little guilt, too. Had he suddenly thought of Mona again?

"How's your house coming along? I hear you and Randolph are quite a couple, too."

Ann's heart slowed as she released her breath with it. For a second it had seemed . . .

"We're like friends," she said firmly. "The same as you and I are friends."

Her gaze was direct as she forced him to turn and look at her. They appraised one another and the silence grew tense.

"What would you say to a cup of coffee?" he asked at last.

"Your place or mine?" she said, laughing.

He laughed, too.

"Well, now that you mention it, how about yours?" he grinned. "From what Christopher tells me you're not far from moving in."

There was a definite look of calculation on his face, which was just about the most roguish, tantalizing thing Ann had ever experienced with a man.

"Why not?" she bantered back. "I was hoping you'd come over and see it soon. There just might be some wine in the cupboard."

He flashed her a look of meaningful anticipation. She smiled back and they easily continued with discussion about construction details. A half hour later he pulled up in front of the domes of her house, which were nearly covered with six feet of earth.

"Wipe your feet," she said with a touch of sternness, as she fiddled with her keys and unlocked the door. "We just laid the carpet this week."

She talked in a rush as the excitement that always accompanies the aromas of a new house assailed her. Nathan laughed, obviously delighted with her effusiveness as he stepped gingerly into the foyer. He was immediately impressed with the fineness of her decorating skills, as the wonderful blend of wallpapers, woods, and modern chandeliers enticed him to the gigantic window wall offset by the huge heat-pack fireplace.

"This is magnificent," he said in honest admiration. His eyes lit on a Persian rug centered before the fireplace and window wall. Several large pillows were scattered and stacked on it. He looked at her musingly, one eyebrow quirked.

She laughed.

"I call that my anticipation spot. I've got new furniture ordered, but it won't be here for a while, so that's where I watch the birds and dream about living here."

Nathan shook his head with just a touch of amused censure.

"Thanks to the windmills I've got electricity and running water," she said, flipping a light on in the kitchen. There was a cozy breakfast nook on the far side of the room. "The bedrooms are down the hall," she said, "and the great room will include dining and outdoor deck areas."

She looked at him expectantly.

"Very interesting and very well done," he said with an affected gentlemanliness.

She gestured toward the nook as she went to a cupboard. "How about a glass of Chianti at room temperature?"

"Bring it on," he said with the widest of grins.

As Ann reached into the cupboard for the wine and

glasses, the intimacy of their surroundings began to affect her and her hands trembled.

Nathan took the straw-covered bottle from her and waited for her to be seated in the wide half-circle booth. The sun streamed around them from another small window wall as he slid in next to her. He took his time pouring the wine and then handed her a glass.

"To you," he said, looking deeply into her eyes, "and to your new home. I hope you'll always be happy here."

She smiled and clinked her glass to his, as a warm rosy glow spread over her. He pressed himself closer to her and put his arm around her. She could feel her thighs molding to his and grew a bit uneasy.

"I want you," he said softly. "I want you more than I've ever wanted anything, right now."

"Nathan," she said, a little bewildered by his directness.

He picked her hands up and pressed one to his mouth. The softness of his caress touched her to her toes.

"The other day," he said.

She saw him swallow as the beginning of a rosy flush spread above the collar of his shirt.

"Forget about the other day," she said.

"Never," he said. "Never."

"Nathan . . ."

She was beginning to feel as if she'd called his name a hundred times and he had yet to hear her.

"I don't understand," she said hesitantly.

"You really touched me the other day," he said sincerely.

Sinkingly she realized she had almost misread him again. It was really mind-boggling to try to keep up with his complexities.

"You know what my problems are, yet I . . . I feel that I need you. The kids like you . . . We all need you."

He swallowed and continued to search her eyes. She held her breath, afraid to speak as he hesitantly went on.

"I really think," he paused, "I've finally begun to adjust to losing Mona . . . and I guess I'm lonelier than ever. Only now it's you I'm thinking about all of the time."

He tipped her chin up and kissed her softly on the lips before she could speak. In just seconds her entire body was molten with yearning as she responded to his touch. He kissed her again, tracing her eyes and caressing her nose as his hands grasped her head firmly and buried themselves in her curly hair. He devoured her mouth and sparred her tongue into submission with his own. His hands moved urgently over her body, pulling her closer.

"Nathan," she breathed, feeling his arms tighten around her.

In one motion he swept her from the booth and carried her toward the Persian rug.

"I want you," he said again, as his lips moved gently down her neck. "And I'm going to love you," he insisted with an unshakable determination, "like you've never been loved. . . ."

Slowly she brought her eyes up to his and matched the pools of yearning she saw there. "I want you, too," she said. "Touch me . . . Touch me softly . . . Yes, like that," she said as he traced her eyes. "Tell me you need me . . . Say my name," she urged.

Slowly and deliberately he nuzzled her ear and sent chills through her as they dropped to the rug. He whispered her name and titillated the tracks around the edges of her ears with his tongue. His hands continued to move gently over her body as they pulled the pillows conveniently around.

Sighing, she pulled him closer until he lay by her side and she moved above him, the aggressor now. His lips moved slowly over her face, her hair, and skin. She could feel gentleness and wonder radiating throughout his great frame. His fingers nimbly unbuttoned her blouse as she lay back languidly, never taking her eyes from his. While she performed the same task for him the passion in his eyes flared and excitement coursed through her. He quickly took in the skimpy low cut of her lacy bra, which hooked in the front, and he freed her breasts with a smooth motion. His mouth moved with hungry urgency towards them. Ann was transported to a state of rapture she'd never imagined possible. He moaned and covered her body with his own, murmuring endearments. Ann knew she wanted him, wanted him more than she'd ever wanted a man before.

Nimbly she began to trail her fingers through the fine soft down on his chest. She outlined his navel and gasped and clung to him in abandoned delight when his warm lips covered her breasts again, moving over them in a natural rhythm. Slowly his lips moved down as she traced his spine and her fingers sent tracks of fire through his loins. They lay bare their entire bodies. Nathan's tongue became a flickering fire dancing over every inch of her skin and her hands reached out to respond with sweet massage.

"Oh, my God," he gasped, as he lay back for a moment of sheer delightful agony. "I can't believe it can be any better." He reached for her and sent his marauding fingers caressing the softness of her inner thigh, moving still higher until she gasped and begged him to give her the final delight.

126

With practiced use of both tongue and hands he brought her entire body to a pitch of exquisite excitement. He merged with her, a great deep spasm sending quivers all the way to her toes. Slowly they rocked, building momentum as he rose above her and swept her away on a powerful sea of sensation.

Her eyes locked with his.

"I love you," she gasped. "I love you . . ."

He gathered her to him as they moved with mutual ecstastic abandon, until at last they both shouted in joyous release.

Gradually their pounding hearts returned to normal and their breathing became steady as they lay happily entwined in each other's arms. Sweetly and softly Nathan began to stroke her in a relaxing sensuous massage. Ann felt an all-enveloping calmness entering every fiber of her being as she began to reciprocate.

"That was wonderful," she said softly. "I don't think I've ever had such an incredible experience."

"And neither have I," Nathan said as he dropped a kiss on her shoulder.

They turned over and relaxed into an easy rapport as they deftly arranged the pillows into a comfortable lounge. The late afternoon sun was streaming through the window wall and gave everything a jungle cast as the outlines of trees and plants splashed over them in shadows.

"How about some more wine?" Nathan asked amiably as he nimbly arose and went toward the breakfast nook.

"Great," said Ann, mesmerized by his graceful, utterly masculine form.

A moment later he was back with bottle and glasses and they settled easily and comfortably into the pillows. They held hands and watched the trees and birds, speaking occasionally in teasing loving banter. They kissed and nuzzled as they watched the sun go down. Their hands retraced their knowledge of one another over and over again. Their eyes met over glasses of wine, they whispered endearments and teased with their bodies until once again they came together in a perfect, utterly fulfilling union, finally falling into a light sleep.

"Thank you, darling Ann," Nathan whispered when they awoke a little later. "I never thought anyone . . ."

As her eyes met his and melted into mutual wells of tenderness she tried to ignore a tiny prickling of uneasiness that curiously responded to his sweet declaration.

He continued to look at her wordlessly for what seemed like an endless moment. He cleared his throat nervously.

"Do you think," he said softly, "we could think about working this out on a more permanent basis?"

She looked at him and took a deep breath. She wanted to be completely sure of his intentions. It mattered too much to her. "Are you talking about marriage, Nathan?"

Her eyes scanned every crevice of his face and moved lingeringly over his lips.

"Well, yes, I guess so," he said.

She could see that he was struggling with the words. She felt as if an eggbeater were scrambling her brain. The room whirled around her and the insidious uneasiness screeched for expression. In spite of her own deep yearning and in spite of the fabulous experience they had just shared, she knew what she must say.

"Nathan . . . I think I'm in love with you and probably nothing in the world would make me happier than becoming your wife, but—"

She looked away, unable to meet his eyes.

"I really don't think you're ready for this yet . . . I don't know for sure if I am."

She felt his body instantly stiffen next to hers.

"We need time," she said gently. "This was wonderful today, but when I marry I want it to be for all the right reasons."

As she groped for words she wondered when she would start hating herself. The truth was she really wanted to stay with him just the way they were, nuptials or no. But her head told her, just as it had through all of her escapades with him, that she had nothing until he accepted her as an individual whom he cared about—not a surrogate for a love he could never have again. She had to be completely sure of that.

She took a sip of wine and felt him beginning to relax.

"Gonna play hard to get, are you?" The mischief was in his eyes again. "Well, all right. If this afternoon is any indication, I think I can give old Randolph a run for his money."

"Nathan," she said, now honestly exasperated, "you are absurd!"

But the softness of his lips as he kissed her gently was anything but that.

CHAPTER NINE

It was well past midnight before Nathan finally left her and the next few days were sheer, heavenly delight as Ann reveled in the memory of their lovemaking. She could feel whispers of approaching autumn. Work on the farms began to gear down. It was the time when farmers traditionally took a short hiatus to make contact with each other before turning their full attention to the fall harvests, when soybeans and corn had to be brought in.

She hadn't seen Nathan since their parting because he had to travel to a national conference on organic farming as a county delegate. But he phoned her every day and Ann was sure they would be making some plans soon. With each passing day she was growing more convinced of his total commitment to her.

Everyone noticed the enchantment that seemed to surround her, but no one spoke directly to her about it except Randolph. In the spirit of their friendship, which both knew was really a comfortable close comradeship and little more, he openly teased her as the final touches neared completion on her underground house.

Everything was perfect except for just a tiny nagging doubt, as Ann still wondered if Nathan had totally resolved his feelings for Mona. But she managed to push it away as she remembered again and again those last wonderful hours with him. She knew, though, beyond a shadow of a doubt, that she loved him and would never be happy with anyone else.

Tanya was also a bit of a problem. It was clear that she had some kind of conflict with the Lost Arts Festival. Although she was always polite, the original spontaneity and warmth was gone. Ann tended to worry over this, but she finally discounted it as nothing serious. Tanya never had been too enthusiastic about household things. Truthfully, with the final details of her house looming before her, Ann really had very little time to dwell on it.

Her parents were ecstatic over the underground house. They came and marveled at the computerized levers which deflected and gathered sunrays and adjusted the angle of the windmill. As they completed piling the earth on top of the inverted domes, Mrs. Taylor insisted that she be allowed to help with the final landscaping.

"Sure, why not?" laughed Ann. "I don't know anyone with a greener thumb than yours, anyway."

"Well, just get a wiggle on then, we've got a lot of work to do. It'll be cold before you know it."

"We," said Ann, laughing all the harder now. "I thought this was going to be your project."

Almost as if too good to be true, the tranquility was shattered when Nathan came storming in her drive. He stepped out of his truck and Ann knew something terrible had happened.

"Nathan," she cried.

Her hand went instinctively to her throat as subconsciously she feared the worst. She thought fleetingly of Tanya and Christopher. Where were they today? Grandpa

Warner? Before her imagination could get completely carried away the suspense was over.

"Damn it to hell!" he said. "I just heard that a big conglomerate is bidding on the rest of the Harding farm and you'll never guess who it is."

"No, never," said Ann, really bewildered now. It was obvious that Nathan's agitation was directed toward her personally.

"Green Valley Farms, that's who," he spit out. "I don't suppose you'd know anything about that!"

Ann's heart fell. Of all the disastrous, impossible coincidences that could have happened, this was absolutely the worst.

"I should have known there was something funny going on," he fumed. "A city girl comes back all humble, taking a cut in pay, and then builds this fancy new house. . . . Why, it couldn't be better. Model house, new test kitchens, all right here together. What did they do? Promise you this house if you could get my land, too? They never start these things unless they have their eye on a big block of land!"

Ann was completely speechless. She never, in her wildest dreams, could have imagined something like this.

"Nathan, I don't know anything about this!"

"Save it," he snarled. "I've only come over here to give you a message. You can send it back to your executive friends. There's not going to be any conglomerate coming in around here. They built you this house for nothing. You can tell them they'll play hell ever getting my land."

He pulled his hat down hard over his head and glared at her. His eyes moved over her derisively and Ann felt that he was committing unholy atrocities upon her entire body. She had never been around such lethal anger.

"Nathan, please," she cried. "You're wrong!"

"We'll just see who's wrong."

He stomped off.

"That's what I'd call a mighty angry man," said Mrs. Taylor.

Ann had almost forgotten her mother was there in her shock.

"Well, daughter," she said, a touch of sternness in her voice, "There isn't anything to what he says, is there?"

"No, of course not!" said Ann. "I don't know about Green Valley Farms coming in, but I certainly don't have anything to do with it. This is as much of a disaster for me as it is for Nathan."

"Well, he's sure got a bee in his bonnet and I don't know how you're going to get this straightened out. Lord knows if he tries to outbid those big guys he'll have to hock everything he's got and then they'll probably just sit back and wait to get it all."

"Oh, Mom, this is awful! We've got to do something."

She was desperate. She couldn't think of anything. She almost died when she thought of the look in Nathan's eyes.

"Maybe if I call them and talk to them . . ."

"I doubt that would do any good," her mother said gloomily. "Sounds to me like the only thing which could save Nathan now is one whole heck of a lot of money."

Money.

The vase.

Ann suddenly thought of the vase. Although it had been just a week since she had sent it off, she'd practically forgotten it.

"Quick, Mom, we've got to get home! I have to use the phone!"

An hour later she was shouting into the phone. The situation had now escalated beyond sane comprehension as she listened to an impersonal voice from the Brant and Tyson Auction Company tell her they knew nothing about the vase she had shipped via special freight the week before.

"But I have the shipping receipt right here in my hand and a letter stating that on the basis of the slides we sent you, you wished to examine it further.

"It's a vase, a valuable antique vase," she finally shouted when questioned as to the exact nature of the article.

"I see," said the deadpan voice, "I'm certain that with the information you have there, we can get this cleared up. Now if you would just go over it with me again."

For the next fifteen minutes Ann described in detail the nature of the vase and all of the procedures she and Randolph had followed. Now and then she heard receivers coming on to the party line and she knew a vast audience was listening to her conversation before she finished.

As she was talking she remembered the fun she and Randolph had had while making all of the arrangements. She also remembered thinking of Nathan as they clicked picture after picture for the slides necessary for the preliminary inquiry. It had been a wonderful lazy day and they had decided to use the windows in the window wall of her house as a background. They had set the vase in the center allowing the natural sunlight to stream about it before zeroing in for close-up detail shots.

All the while she had been remembering the couple who had once owned this vase and kept it as a very personal keepsake. There were still petals from dried flowers in the bottom. She had been looking forward to seeing Nathan and driving to the Amish settlement. At the same time she was enjoying an incredible warm camaraderie with Randolph as they joked and fussed over just the right way to take the pictures. It was funny. She knew she was in love with Nathan now, but her friendship with Randolph was important, too.

As she hung up the phone just one word pulsed through her mind. Incredible. This was just incredible! She had to get over to Nathan's and make him understand.

She made a quick call to Randolph to enlist his help with the vase and then grabbed her purse and ran for the car. She realized in her desperation that she had really hoped to have something wonderful to tell Nathan about the vase.

Really, she thought to herself, *you can't go around dealing with pipe dreams, either.* No. Before she saw Nathan again perhaps she'd better try to get to the bottom of this rumor about the Green Valley Farms. Quickly she returned to the house and dialed the offices of her previous employer in Chicago.

"Harry," she said, as the voice of her old supervisor came onto the phone, "I've just been told the most impossible thing."

Harry quickly directed her to the proper officials for her inquiry and the evasive, broad, noncommittal answers she received to her questions left her suspecting the very worst.

"But why," she asked in desperation, "would you be interested in just a few hundred acres?"

"Well, of course, Ann, you understand that this is really an amazing coincidence. Nothing is firm yet. As you know our overall expansion policies are subject to extensive long-range planning . . ."

Ann heard receivers clicking on the line again and with

a sinking feeling realized she may have just sealed the suspicions everyone already had. The whole community would soon know she had been in contact with Green Valley Farms and there was no doubt in her mind that their interpretation of this call could be disastrous.

Chaos was courting her. Murphy's law was badgering her. She was going from bad to worse. She took a deep breath. *You've got to get your wits together,* she said to herself. *Your initial instinct was right. Go and talk to Nathan.*

A drizzle had begun to come down when she drove into the Warner yard. It was a fitting setting for the gloom in her heart. She went up and knocked on the door hesitantly and was greeted by a beaming Grandpa Warner.

"Come in, come in," he said.

She smiled, grateful for the spark his spirit provided.

"I've come to see Nathan," she said hesitantly.

"Oh, he's out in the barn," he said. "I expect you can find him there."

"Thanks," she said, grateful for more than just the information. The old man's friendly demeanor had done much to calm her fears. She had a feeling she was blowing this all out of proportion. All she needed to do was explain this to Nathan rationally. He was too intelligent to be unreasonable.

As she stepped into the barn she was again instantly reminded of that first intimate session she had enjoyed with Nathan here. It seemed like ages ago. They had come down a long road together since then and had sampled such incredible comfort and understanding of one another during that time. For weeks everything had been wonderful, until this morning. She couldn't believe Nathan could throw away all of that intimate trust and friendship.

raise her own voice now, "have you actually discussed this with the realtor? Do you really know what's going on?"

"I know what's going on," he said. "I know that some damned bunch of big businessmen who don't give a hoot for the land or anything that grows on it is coming in to ruin what little is left of the farms around here!"

She looked at him and realized that everything she had ever yearned for was being destroyed right in front of her eyes. This agitated, demonic man was a complete stranger to her. His unreasonableness was overwhelming. She could feel a pain moving slowly in the wake of her earlier fear and anxiety and it was going to completely destroy any hope they might have ever had for one another.

"Nathan," she said softly. "I thought we had something special. . . . I thought it was going to grow."

She stepped up to him and forced herself to touch his rigid angry body. She blanched when she felt his instinctive recoil.

Resolutely she went on. "I wouldn't do anything to harm you or any of your family. I love all of you. You know I do. I've never been closer to or given more of myself to a man." Her voice was barely audible. "I love you, Nathan."

For just a moment her eyes met his and she saw just a spark of the warmth and love they had once shared. For just a second his lips wavered and then she saw the shade of obstinacy come down hard and tight. He brought his arms up and drew back.

"Look," she said with a sigh, "I know you don't believe me. You're too upset to believe me now, but I'm going to tell you something anyway and when you finally screw your head on again it might make some sense to you."

She took a big breath and looked him square in the eyes.

"I don't want to see Green Valley Farms come in here any more than you do and I don't want to see you lose your farm or anything else like that. On an outside chance that your vase just might be very valuable I called the auction firm and I've just learned that there has been some mix-up there, too, so I've called Randolph to help me. I know all of this sounds crazy, but believe me, if there's anything we can do to help you keep those people out, we're going to do it. If by some miracle the vase is valuable you could have more than enough to buy that land. I'm sure of it."

She had spoken very calmly and firmly, but he just went on looking at her in a cold, unseeing way.

"Right now I've got to find out what's happened to the vase, but I have shipping receipts and slides, so I'm sure we can get it cleared up. Believe me, Nathan, I have nothing to do with Green Valley now."

"If that's the case," said Tanya's caustic voice as she came in, "why were you just on the phone to them?"

Nathan's head snapped and she saw all of his anger return.

"Reporting in and getting instructions?" he snarled.

"No, Nathan, no," she sighed, "but if that's what you want to believe, I guess there's nothing I can do about it."

She looked at Tanya, surprised and hurt by this unexpected attack. She had honestly thought the young girl was her friend. She turned in total dejection and walked away. She could feel tears behind her eyelids and she dared not look back lest Nathan see how badly they had hurt her. If she had, she would have seen him slump, too, as his arms reached out emptily.

He swallowed hard as Tanya continued with her diatribe. "Dad, you were right. She was just on the phone

140

checking to see what they were doing next and then she *has* got something going on with that vase, too. She's probably trying to steal that from you, too."

"That's enough, Tanya," said Nathan sternly, but Ann was already out of earshot, in her car, getting ready to leave. "You know better than to make accusations based on gossip. What's got into you?"

"But, Dad!"

"Forget it," he said. "Maybe I've said too much, too. I don't know. . . . I just don't know."

There was an incredible sadness in his voice.

As Ann drove down the road she was blinded by hot tears. *Whatever had made her think,* she thought vehemently, *that she had anything in common with such an unreasonable man?*

She wasn't angry. She was drained, almost as if the very essence of life had been taken from her. All their time together . . . All their sharing . . . All their intimacy . . . She had bared her soul to him. It meant nothing.

Nathan had immediately thought the worst of her and then refused, after she had practically begged him to believe her, to show her some consideration. No matter what happened now, she knew it was over between them. Nothing could ever make it right again.

CHAPTER TEN

The scandal swirled throughout the community and for a time Ann despaired that even her job might be affected. For several days she received calls not only at home, but at work as well. It was amazing how vindictive people could be on nothing more than the merest wisp of gossip. Fortunately the scope of her work was countywide and her family and work associates were soon aware of the actual facts and offered her their total support. The main flurry of the controversy was centered in her local community, only a small pocket of her overall territory.

The Lost Arts Festival changed from an event Ann had anticipated with pleasure to something she dreaded as she labored through the final preparations. She was not sure how she might be treated by the public and she was still numb from her encounter with Nathan and Tanya. Emotionally she just wasn't strong enough to confront Tanya again so she had just gone on without her. The majority of the work was completed. The setup of the booth was really the only major thing left.

After leaving the Warner farm, Ann had felt her own shade come down over her body as she sought protection from her emotions. The thought of any further bruising was just insufferable. She was like a zombie moving among scraps of wood and other mess as the final touches to the booth constructed on Main Street were completed. She was standing on a ladder about to fasten some bunting when, to her surprise, Tanya arrived.

"Tanya?" she queried.

Tanya was carrying a large box and there was a sulky look on her face as she mumbled what sounded like a halfhearted greeting.

"Where do you want me to put this?" she asked.

Ann could not hide her own confusion as she stopped in midmotion.

"Really, Tanya, you don't have to do this. I understand perfectly."

"No, you don't," she said. "I made a promise and Warners always meet their responsibilities."

"Certainly I understand that," said Ann in exasperation, "but I don't expect you to do something that is obviously distasteful to you. Neither of us would enjoy that!"

As she spoke she had begun to punctuate her words with her hands and suddenly she lost her footing and began to topple from the ladder.

"Whoa there!" said a deep voice, as strong hands came up and encircled her waist. She fell back on a broad chest. She was immediately enveloped by a strong masculine scent, the memory of which had haunted her. As she looked into Nathan's eyes there was no way she could mask the confusion in her own. It was mirrored in his, too. But his eyes were also wells of pain as he searched her face before setting her down gently.

"Tanya has something she wants to say," he said slowly. He looked at his daughter meaningfully.

The young girl looked at the ground and finally met Ann's eyes defiantly.

"I'm sorry," she said. "I shouldn't have said the things that I did the other day. I didn't know what I was talking about. I heard something on the phone . . ."

She looked away.

Ann regretted that with every word of apology the young girl was cementing her hatred toward her. But she also knew that it was not her place to interfere any further with Nathan and his children.

"Don't worry about it, Tanya," she said softly. "We all make mistakes sometimes."

The young woman showed little response.

"And don't worry about the booth. Everything is really just about taken care of."

"No," said Tanya stubbornly. "I made a commitment and I'll keep it. Now just tell me what to do."

Not wanting any further scenes Ann looked at Nathan menacingly, took a deep breath, and decided to make the most of it, although she definitely did not appreciate the tense atmosphere that was all about them.

"Very well," she sighed. "We need to get the posters and bunting up and then start to organize the items for both the display and the demonstrations."

"Here, I'll give a hand, too," said Nathan, as he started up the ladder she had just toppled from.

"That's not neccessary," said Ann.

"Oh, but it is," he said softly.

His eyes engaged hers and she could feel her temper rising. *Was a simple apology from him, too, really so impossible?* She willfully projected her thoughts and saw him flush in confusion. Then a big smile spread over his face and Ann knew it would do no good to argue with him now. Besides she really wasn't up to it and what did it matter anyway. There would never be anything between them again. She was sure of that.

She worked in virtual silence except for giving terse instructions or answering questions with clipped, short replies. The uneasiness between her and Tanya was thick and unnerving, but Nathan seemed to be impervious to the tensions swirling around him as he joked and bantered. He called out to people and in general carried on as though everything were fine. It was as if the entire episode concerning the Harding farm had never happened.

As the day wore on Ann attempted to demonstrate different items in preparation for the actual show the next day. Nathan never went far from the booth. His boisterous spirits were evident to everyone and his presence certainly couldn't be missed. When Randolph arrived a little later his amazement matched Ann's and that of quite a few other people who were passing by. Had it not been for Tanya's barely concealed somber attitude, Ann might have been affected, too, as the infectiousness of Nathan's charm snared person after person.

As the day wore on the tension began to give Ann a nagging headache. She decided to take a break and grabbed an old wooden water bucket which she planned to fill with water. As she examined it the vase again came to her mind. The auction firm was still giving her trouble and she knew she had to get that straightened out, too. She needed to rid herself of the entire entanglement with the Warners. After today, she knew for her own sanity that she couldn't take very much more of this. She didn't know what Nathan's game was, but he could count her out.

When she returned, in spite of her resolve not to react or feel, anger began to build in her. It was obvious now

145

that Nathan was putting on a show, letting people know that nothing serious had happened between them. As she screwed down the paddle of an old cheese press each turn became an act of vengeance.

Coming out here and putting on this show, forcing Tanya to accompany him when he's not even man enough to call me up and make a simple apology, let alone listen to me in the first place!

As she began to arrange the display she could feel herself grow rigid with anger every time Nathan maneuvered to be near her. When she resolutely pounded the spikes of an antique meat tenderizer, she came to within inches of his fingers as he stood grinning, not for one moment intimidated by her temper or actions.

While a general hustle and bustle went on around them, Tanya, Randolph, and the other helpers all seemed to suddenly disappear and the two of them were alone. The drawn-out silence created an unbearable tension between them. Nathan looked at her and swallowed hard, but his eyes commanded that she respond as he stepped close to her.

"The other day you said you loved me . . ."

His voice was barely audible.

Ann thought she was hearing things.

"I . . . don't know what you're talking about," she sputtered, but her hand went involuntarily to her breast as she willed her wildly beating heart to be still.

"I know it's going to take time," he went on. "I know this isn't the place. It's just that I don't know any other way. I didn't think you would see me."

Ann was really, for the first time in her life, totally speechless. She knew she was imagining this.

"It's just that," he went on, "I want you to know that I have got things straightened out now. . . ."

He swallowed again.

"I know now that what was important in the past is past . . . And what's important today is you. I love you, Ann."

Nathan's face was a plane of agony, but Ann simply could not comprehend what he was saying. Before she could muster any kind of reply they were surrounded by people again. She saw Nathan assume his familiar relaxed air, but not before he scanned her, beseeching her, and then looked away when he saw her lack of response.

Ann was so unnerved now that she wasn't sure about anything, but she did know that it wasn't going to be that easy. No way. She was unconsciously working with an ugly old grater. As she turned the crank its jagged teeth whirled around in fitting accompaniment to her emotions.

Nathan continued to glance at her. She turned her back resolutely and began to occupy herself with a stoneware churn. Her fingers moved over the smooth glazed surface and the radiant picture of the young missionaries, who had had such a wonderful, understanding relationship, flashed in front of her. She felt her back stiffen board-straight as her resolve returned fully. *That's what I want,* she grimaced. *Nothing more and nothing less.*

She set the churn aside and reached for an old-fashioned ice cream freezer, which was just a box inside of a box with a crank. She looked up and smiled at Randolph as he returned to her side, but she felt a chill entering her soul and she knew that the days ahead were not going to be easy.

She went on setting up an old wooden sausage grinder and tried to figure out the wild mechanisms of a butter worker and felt again a surge of relief as she worked the parts of a bottle corker, pushing it vigorously up and down. As she labored, a certain rhythm seemed to develop and she found her mind growing rather peaceful.

She wondered if the young missionary wife had ever had times when just the exercise of physical living had been her therapy. *No,* she thought, *with love like theirs they never knew what it was like to hurt one another.*

Nathan was still hovering in the background, but Ann refused to look at him. *How dare he come in here in such a way!* In just a few months he had done more to shake up her life, to unsettle her down to her very soul, than anyone she had ever known. Now, overnight, after treating her in the most horrendous, cavalier way she could possibly imagine, he thought one word from him and everything was going to be all right. *Never!*

After a while it was apparent that Nathan's ploy had more than worked as people came by, chatty and friendly, and exclaimed over the exhibit. *But then,* she thought, *maybe a lot of that was just my imagination.* Her dad had said most people didn't pay much attention to the busybodies. She wasn't going to give Nathan more credit than he deserved. At the bottom line he still hadn't been man enough to just plain apologize! *But then,* she thought as another insidious suspicion began to take form, *what if, in his heart, he still thinks I have something to do with the Green Valley bid. He might actually think I was trying to steal the vase!*

No. This thing wasn't over yet. It wasn't cleared up. Knowing Nathan, his innate decency would have driven him to do what he had done today. It was more than obvious to the discerning soul that the gossip was out of hand and overembellished. He wouldn't have wanted to be a part of that.

She had to do something to get this straightened out. She set an old scale on the counter and looked for its weights. Justice was still far away. *But,* a little voice insisted from deep inside, *he just said he loved you!*

No way, she responded, *no way.*

She knew how deep-seated his emotions were about Mona. He couldn't have resolved them so quickly. No, he was still angry and suspicious. She knew it now. He had to be. This whole thing was just some ploy of his. It was as clear as could be and she wasn't going to allow herself to trust him.

She turned and took another deep breath. She saw him watching from afar and she could see the calculating gleam in his eyes now. She turned away again and realized that it was imperative that she get that vase back and sever all ties. The sooner the better.

The next day the festival went off without a hitch and Tanya even began to warm up a little before it was all over. Ann, however, remained wary, relaxing only when her parents and Grandpa Warner came by and she was still no match for Christopher and his indomitable spirit.

He had come in with his hip adolescent chatter, absconded with three dollars of her money for some raffle tickets, going off with a wave as he asked her to watch him perform again that evening. He and Randolph were her bright spots and she truly enjoyed the chat she had with Dale Spencer about the music project when he happened by.

"Looks like we might be able to schedule one of Christopher's competitions for this winter," he said, as he gave a wave to leave, "but I'll get back to you on that."

Ann smiled and waved back and then turned to see Nathan ever in the background. His eyes never seemed to leave her and she was acutely uncomfortable now whenever he was around. She had not spoken directly to him since his surprising declaration of the day before. He seemed to be avoiding her, too, now that he had had his say and gone out of his way to unnerve her.

She would be glad when this was all over so she wouldn't have to subject herself to any more of this harassment. She supposed she could have told him to get lost, but she felt they were already enough of a spectacle in the community. She didn't need any more attention from her neighbors.

It seemed like only hours when in reality it had been days since the Lost Arts Festival. Ann had almost forgotten what a taskmaster her mother could be as Ann went about the landscaping of her new home while at the same time attending to the responsibilities of her job. Now she sat totally exhausted at the FFA barbecue chicken booth at the county fair, barely tasting her food.

She noticed a general movement toward the stock barn area and sensed a growing air of excitement.

"By damn, there's a real duel goin' on over there," said a grizzled farmer as he plopped himself down to a plate of chicken, beans, and potato salad.

"What do you mean?" asked the attendant.

"That Warner girl is over there battling it out for Grand Champion against the Hebert boy. Those cows are so well matched I think it's gonna be decided on showmanship. Judge can't make up his mind!"

Ann was interested in spite of herself.

She finished her lunch and got up with a sigh. Before she knew it she was heading for the barns. There was a crowd around the show ring and the sun was broiling everything. As she skirted the edge of the congregation she saw Tanya and several other young people clad in white patiently leading big, beautifully groomed Holstein heifers around the ring. Sweat was pouring from Tanya's brow and the black and white coat of her animal glistened in the sun.

The judge had placed six other entries, but he was obviously stymied over the last two contestants. The Hebert boy had a big, unruly heifer, which he obviously controlled with an iron hand. The animals were both perfect specimens of the breed and it was obvious that Tanya was in a real battle.

Ann began to move up through the crowd as she kept her eyes glued on the young girl. Tanya's heifer was beautifully trained and obviously very docile as she responded easily to both the judge and her master. As the cow took up the majestic hind foot forward, front feet firmly planted pose, she chewed her cud as though unaware of anything going on around her.

Ann bumped into someone.

"Oh, I beg your pardon," she said.

"Not at all," said an amused voice.

Her head snapped up and she met Nathan's smiling eyes.

"She's wonderful, isn't she?" he said, motioning to Tanya.

"Yes," said Ann, flustered in spite of her resolve.

As they watched, the judge walked around Tanya's heifer again and then reached for his handkerchief to wipe his brow. He stuffed it halfheartedly back into his rear pocket. Both the young man and Tanya were grim with concentration. It was obvious that showmanship was going to make a difference in this instance. The judge turned away and began to examine the hindquarters and udder of the Hebert entry when suddenly the entire crowd gasped. Tanya's cow had noted the waving handkerchief in the judge's pocket and nonchalantly broke her pose to reach out and grab it with her long tongue.

Ann's heart went out to Tanya as she saw the young girl's face plummet. The judge turned around, a look of surprise on his face, and Tanya knew it was all over.

He smiled as titters went through the crowd, gave both animals a final pat, and went over to the table. As the silence grew he shuffled through some papers and then seemed to be examining what looked to Ann like 4-H project books.

He heaved a little sigh and pursed his face in a final grimace. Ann could almost feel the nearness of Nathan as they both stood stock-still in breathless anticipation. Ann saw Tanya glance at her father and saw him give her a little nod of encouragement. Tanya managed a little smile in return.

Ann could feel her heart beginning to beat as she tried to manuever away. Before she managed two steps a strong arm reached out and drew her into a casual hug.

"Don't leave now," he whispered in her ear. "Tanya needs all the support she can get."

She flushed as she physically responded to the nearness of his lips, the sensation of his warm breath on her skin. Others were beginning to glance at them so she just stood quietly, not saying a word to him.

The judge stepped to the microphone.

"Ladies and gentlemen, I don't think I've ever had a harder time making up my mind. These two young people are a fine example of good 4-H programs and they are a credit to their community."

Ann could see that Tanya was holding her breath and there was a hint of tears as the spectacle of the handkerchief hovered in her consciousness.

"I think, though,"—Ann heard the judge say through a haze—"I have to go with the young lady!"

A whoop went up in the crowd and Tanya's face was a wreath of disbelief as she lit up in happy smiles.

Quickly the judge placed the two animals and went to get the big rosette ribbons and trophies.

"I want you to know," he went on, as the presentations were being made, "the animals are identical in quality, care, and grooming. Showmanship was not a factor. One of the animals is very relaxed and the other obviously is a little more unruly, but with the champion's little handkerchief escapade they evened out again. I have a feeling that someone carries a lot of goodies in her pockets!"

A laugh went through the crowd and Ann found herself laughing along with Nathan and Tanya in sheer relief.

"No, I finally made my decision based on the overall 4-H project of these young people. Again it was hard, but when I saw the shrewdness with which this young lady must have chosen this heifer as a calf from blood lines that weren't that rich compared to the lineage of the other cow here, and the way she developed and trained her animal, I think that she deserves the distinction of 4-H Grand Champion. I salute you, Tanya Warner, as a fine farmer."

Tanya was beaming and it was obvious that she was at last receiving the recognition she had sought for so long from her dad as well as the public. As she emerged from the throng of well-wishers and headed for the barn Ann and Nathan followed along.

Ann was so excited that she never gave a thought to what she was doing. It just seemed natural to move along with Nathan as he shook hands and clapped friends on the back in his obvious joy over his daughter's victory. When they finally reached Tanya he went to her and swooped her into his arms in a big hug.

"Oh, Dad," she cried, "I thought I'd really blown it. I only relaxed for a second."

"You were wonderful, honey. Don't worry about it. You know," he went on, "I think you're one hell of a farmer, too."

Father and daughter looked at one another in a wonderful communion and Ann knew a marvelous understanding and recognition had just occurred. She was sincerely happy for them, but she felt like an intruder.

"Ann always said you were the real farmer in the family," said Nathan as he drew Ann in.

Tanya looked at Ann with a funny expression.

Realizing that she had just managed to involve herself with these people again, Ann was suddenly self-conscious and wanted to extricate herself from this situation as soon as possible.

"Do you mean," she heard Tanya asking, "that you were trying to get Dad to understand that I'm serious about the farm?"

There was an undeniable softening about her.

"I think maybe," Tanya said, looking at the ground, "I've been a real dip, haven't I? I knew you were just trying to help us with the vase and all . . . but somehow when Dad got all excited about me working with those kitchen things I began to think you were against my being a farmer too. That you were trying to get me interested in 'woman's' things and I was sure you and Dad were in cahoots. Then when Dad got so upset and I heard that gossip . . ." Her voice trailed off.

She looked up and Ann saw real affection in her eyes.
"I'm sorry," she said. "I'm really sorry."

"I understand," said Ann as she went to her and gave her a hug. "Really I do. Congratulations. You were wonderful today."

"Yes, she was," said Nathan, "and it was really wonderful that you were here to see it."

She met his eyes and looked away.

"Yes, well . . . I have a lot of work to do," she said quickly. "I just wanted to say hello."

She turned and walked away, but she could feel two pairs of very troubled eyes following her progress. She straightened her back and walked resolutely on, but not before Christopher caught up with her and began to regale her with an account of Tanya's victory.

Against her will he hustled her right back to the spot she had just left. As general happy hoopla continued to go on around the stall where the cow was tied, she found herself confronting the demanding eyes of Nathan again.

He stood silently and watched her now, but it made no difference. She wasn't going to change her mind. The entire family was soon there and Ann finally took her leave quietly. She refused to look back.

As she walked away she realized there was just one item of unfinished business between her and Nathan—the vase. She still had to find it, but in the meantime she never wanted to meet Nathan's eyes or touch him again. Her response to him was far too insidious.

CHAPTER ELEVEN

Within a few weeks it was all straightened out. Green Valley Farms had indeed made an inquiry about the Harding farm, but for their purposes it was really much too small a holding. They were far more interested in the land farther north where they might have the chance to consolidate thousands of acres. When they investigated the surrounding area they moved their sights further on.

It was a hollow victory for Ann. Fortunately she had been very busy with moving into her new home along with catching up on her work after the fair. Randolph had continued to provide her with a warm friendship and was in many ways her salvation.

The weather was bleak and matched her spirit completely. She was sitting by the window wall, a lonely silhouette next to the roaring fireplace. Warm slacks and a downy sweater gave her a comfortable appearance as she pulled her legs up. She wanly smiled at the greedy antics of the cardinals and other birds fighting over the goodies in the feeders she had placed about. Snow flurries were beginning to tease as the end of fall gave way to winter.

In spite of herself she began to think of Nathan and was immediately enveloped in an unbearable pain. She jumped as the doorbell broke into her reverie. She wasn't expecting anyone. With the weather so threatening she was sure Randolph would not be coming up.

She got up with a languid grace and fluffed her hair as she went to the door. Her eyes were aghast as they lit on the big, lonely huddled figure in front of her.

"Nathan!"

She was too surprised to say anything else.

"May I come in?" he asked.

There was a deep moroseness about him, but she steeled herself against any normal reactions she might have felt. There was a cold hardness in her eyes as she opened the door wide and motioned for him to come in.

"I see your house has turned out very well," he said. He looked around appreciatively, but she refused to allow her eyes to meet his.

"Is something wrong?" she asked rather dispassionately. "Are the cows out again?"

"No, no," he said, attempting a little smile. "No . . . I . . . ah, came over to see you."

"You might have called."

"Well, yes, I suppose so, but I was just coming by . . ."

She had no intention of making this easy for him. "Well?"

"Could we sit down?" he asked as he looked about her big spacious great room.

"Will it take that long?"

Her eyes were dead and cold, but she could feel the beginning of an insidious stirring as she pursed her lips and resolved to see this through.

"Yes, it might," he said firmly.

She felt something flip-flop inside of her and she knew she was in trouble.

"All right then. Let me have your coat."

He immediately began to shrug out of it. When she reached for it his nearness was like a heady summer breeze full of alfalfa, clover, and spicy after-shave lotion. Her fingers inadvertently grazed the muscles in his arm and she knew she was going to have to be more than just careful.

"I . . . I . . . got this letter from the Brant and Tyson Auction Company. It seems they have records showing they did receive a vase from you, but they can't identify it now."

She looked at him wordlessly as he sat down while apparently choosing his words carefully.

"I guess you must have told them to get in touch with me."

She remained silent.

"Well, it's probably not worth anything anyway, but the truth is I wouldn't recognize it if I saw it."

She looked at him and gauged her words very carefully.

"Well, in that case, why even bother?"

He looked to the floor with a grimace.

"Look, I know I've got this coming," he said finally.

"You've got nothing coming, Nathan," she said, her face stern and eyes wide. "I don't know what you're talking about."

"I really blew it, didn't I?"

"Yes."

"There's nothing more to say?"

"No."

She didn't dare attempt anything more than her terse replies. Already her body was beginning to feel dusky as she felt her color rising above the cowl of her sweater. She was grateful that the light was dim and the fire was the only illumination.

"I guess I may as well go then," he said with a grimace.

"Guess so," she echoed.

She went to get his coat and willed her legs not to shake as the rest of her body rose up and threatened total betrayal. But then she remembered his cutting, unreasonable accusations fueled by Tanya's caustic barbs. In spite of the touching scene at the fair she was still affected by it. Her pride cemented her resolve firmly into place.

"Well, the reason I came over . . . I was wondering if you would go with me to check out the vase. But seeing how you feel, maybe you could just go and let me pick up the tab."

She was stunned. He could be most persistent when he wanted to be. In a way it was almost flattering, but she had to stand firm. Her voice trembled. "I'd really have to think about that. I don't know what my plans are. I'll have to check my calendar."

She could feel herself wavering and looked defiantly away.

He looked at her with an uncanny expression. As he buttoned his coat he reached out and lightly caressed her cheek. He turned her chin and his eyes looked into hers.

"I'm sorry," he said softly.

He pulled his hat down snug and went out the door.

Ann stood still for a full minute staring at the closed door. Slowly she brought her hand to her face and then she crumpled into tears.

"Nathan!" she called as she flung the door open. But her words were whipped away by the wind and he was gone.

She turned and went back into the room, where she huddled on the couch. She was being ridiculous. She knew she was. He didn't deserve any consideration from her. He had shown her anything but consideration, almost from their first moment of meeting.

She thought back over their entire tempestuous relationship and realized it was more appropriate for a soap opera than real life. First his preoccupation with his late wife, Mona, her own grief for Jeff, his stubborn resistance to Christopher's musical aspirations, his dedication to the land and farming, and then finally his acid accusations and total unreasonableness.

In her quest to touch a very special soul she had suffered more insult and abuse than any one person should ever have to experience. It wasn't that she wasn't capable of forgiving Nathan. The feelings she was having right now told her that was more than possible. She had glimpsed the sensitive, complicated inner man who was the real Nathan Warner on many occasions and she could fully understand the depth of feelings which could drive a man to act the way he had. What she could never accept, or begin to live with, was his total lack of trust in that crucial moment of adversity.

She sighed as she went into her kitchen to prepare a cup of herb tea. She looked around and thought of all the wonderful moments she had spent with Randolph in planning and building this perfect nest. Almost as if on cue, Jeff, too, came to mind.

"You have certainly created a complicated life for yourself," she said out loud.

She smiled as Oscar, a big cat who had decided to take up residence with her, came in and demanded his dinner.

"That's right," she said. "All I need is one more difficult male in my life."

As she spoke she knew what she was going to do. It was

160

crazy and she should know better, but she stepped to the phone anyway.

"Christopher, this is Ann," she said seconds later. "Tell your dad I'll help him with the vase."

She hung up, afraid to say more.

They got together on a hushed and frozen Friday, the day after Thanksgiving. A perfect mantle of snow covered everything. When she heard his car coming up the lane Ann had put her coat on and was out the door before Nathan could alight from his car.

"Brr," she chattered, scurrying into the car. "Are you sure you want to make this trip all the way to Cleveland today?"

"Sure," he grinned, as he reached across to help her pull the car door closed.

His arm brushed the front of her coat and it would have been an intimate gesture if she hadn't been so bundled up. The car was warm and the tail pipe spewed forth a white stream, giving the enclosure a snug intimacy in the unreal winter landscape.

"It's so quiet here," he said, as he straightened next to her. His lips were only inches from her face. "Beautiful," he went on reverently. "I always love the first snow of the year, don't you?"

His eyes were liquid pools surrounded by his soft voice.

"Yes," said Ann, as she felt that insidious rush again, "but we'd better get going. We want to be sure and get back tonight."

"By all means," he said with a hint of impudence. "Heaven forbid that we should spend a night together."

Her eyes snapped in an immediate response, but she said nothing. Nathan frowned and looked away, as he

161

gunned the motor and slowly made his way out of her lane.

"Have you got the slides and papers?" he asked moments later, as they pulled out onto the slushy highway. All vestiges of his momentary impatience were gone.

"Yes," she said as she patted her voluminous purse. "Right here."

"Great," he said.

He reached over and switched the radio on. The soft sounds of an FM station quickly enveloped them and again Ann had the feeling of being in an ethereal cocoon. She sighed and sat back, allowing her hand to trail on the seat next to his knee.

"Did you have a nice Thanksgiving?" she asked conversationally.

"Sure did," he said with a smile. "Christopher just outdid himself."

It was uncanny. That night after her call to Christopher, Nathan had called back and they had very matter-of-factly planned this trip. Now it was almost as if they'd never been estranged. They were just neighbors talking over the fence. Well, almost. Now and then they both fell into silence as they searched for other safe topics to discuss. There would be a burst of words and then an awkward moment. They exhausted every conceivable comment with reference to the weather, their families, and her new house. Finally Nathan just gripped the wheel and drove as they entered the big interstate heading for Cleveland.

"I really do appreciate your doing this for me."

He glanced at her, and Ann could see that he was sincere.

"No problem," she responded as she turned and looked

out at the blustery landscape. She felt something akin to the chill outside, but somehow the tension seemed to ease and they both settled more naturally into their surroundings. Both grew quiet and introspective.

Ann leaned back again and the warmth of the car seemed to meld with the music, drawing their bodies closer together. The strains of a song suddenly seemed to surge and reach out to them as a strong voice sang of love and loss.

Nathan looked at her. Hesitantly his hand reached out and began to creep toward hers. She felt the touch of his fingers, and then gradually his hand covered hers, sending pain through her from head to toe.

"No, Nathan, no," she sighed.

She looked to the ceiling and felt herself growing dizzy while the world whirled by on the outside, but she made no move to retract her hand. She felt his gaze lingering and questioning as he juggled his driving with his inquiry. Finally, as the strains of the song ended, he lifted his hand, leaving hers cold and bare. She went on gazing out the windows as the music continued to feed the vibrations in the car. She could feel tears welling behind her eyes and she had to muster all of her resources to control them. She was beginning to feel this trip was a terrible mistake.

"Cup of coffee?"

She gave a little start.

Nathan was gesturing toward a big truck stop sign.

"Yes," she said, obvious relief in her voice. "I think we could use a break."

Again she could sense his questioning glance, but somehow there was also a sense of patience—an indefatigable patience. It left her with a strange feeling. She honestly didn't know if she felt glad or threatened.

The rest of the trip after their coffee took little more than an hour. They managed to settle into an easy, mundane conversation, and soon they were in the sloppy, busy traffic of downtown Cleveland.

As they walked into the posh meeting room of the big hotel where the auction was being held as a benefit for a local charity, they were transported into another world. Ann knew it was going to be strange when she spied two monstrous, ugly iron dogs guarding the entrance. When they walked through the door she could sense Nathan's unease in this Alice in Wonderland hodgepodge. It matched her own. Elegantly dressed women greeted them cordially and in polished, hushed voices explained that there was still time to browse about before the auction began. One insisted that they register while she handed them a strange-looking card with a number.

"Use that if you want to bid on anything and let us know if there's anything you're particularly interested in—"

"Really, that's not neccessary," said Ann as she began fumbling with her purse. "We're here to see Mr. Harold Baker about an Oriental vase we sent to him for an appraisal."

"Well, I'm sure he's here someplace," said the woman. "In the meantime perhaps you'd like to just look around or enjoy some wine and cheese."

She gestured toward a bar and appetizer area set up a little farther away.

Ann looked at Nathan.

"Sure," he said. "Maybe we'll be able to spot what we're looking for." He looked a little bewildered.

There was a rather hushed atmosphere, similar to that of a funeral parlor, as they walked gingerly about the room. Not too many people were there yet and everyone seemed to be speaking in low voices or whispers. The room was a wild myriad of colors. Huge Persian and Oriental rugs covered the walls and every imaginable kind of bric-a-brac, artwork, jewelry, and glassware were displayed. Ann really wasn't sure about the pieces of antique furniture around the room. These were obviously the effects of many wealthy estates, but for the life of her, Ann couldn't squelch a feeling of walking through an incredible, ornate flea market as they picked their way around the room.

"For heaven's sake, Nathan, whatever you do, don't raise that card when the auction starts. I'd hate to think of buying any of this stuff."

He laughed, honestly amused by her reaction, and seemed to relax.

One of the most ludicrous things in the room was a huge stuffed boa constrictor, coiled like a giant cobra, rising more than six feet from its wooden platform. A candlestick was mounted on its head.

"Now that's just what you need," said Nathan affably.

"No, thank you," she said, as she smiled and began to honestly enjoy herself.

"Well, how about this?" said Nathan, as they stepped to the jewelry cases where armed guards hovered in the background. He was pointing to a small oval pin encrusted with diamonds. "Would something like that make you happy?"

He smiled and gave her arm a little squeeze.

Before they could stop him the attendant behind the case was unlocking the door and bringing the pin out to show it off on a velvet cloth.

"Yes, it's lovely," said Ann a little uneasily.

"The price is right, too," said the smiling man. "Only fourteen thousand, appraised value."

Nathan nodded, feigning nonchalance, but Ann had felt his intake of breath.

"I see," she said mischievously.

She smiled and resisted an impulse to tease Nathan as she fingered the bidding card.

"Really, we're just browsing," she said. "Actually we're looking for Mr. Baker. Could you possibly direct us to him?"

"Yes, he's right over there," the man said, gesturing across the room.

Ann followed his gesture and could see that the man was engrossed in conversation with another couple, but at least they had identified him.

During their leisurely stroll around the room the volume of chatter had steadily risen as the room filled with people. The ambience was now more that of a cocktail party as patrons stood with wineglasses and cigarettes while they pleasantly discussed different items.

As they moved closer to Mr. Baker, Ann could see that there were some very lovely items as well as numerous things she found tasteless and gauche. She was just examining a lovely decanter when her eye fell on the vase. She was sure it was the one that belonged to Nathan.

"Nathan!" she whispered as she tugged on his sleeve like a little girl. "I see it! Over there!"

She was pointing excitedly.

It was obvious that Mr. Baker was discussing it also as he stepped over and picked it up so the couple with him could examine it more closely. Ann stood in total agitation as she tried to think of a polite way to get his attention. Finally the couple stepped away and with a nod of his head Mr. Baker took the vase with him toward the front of the room.

"Mr. Baker," called Ann as she rushed after him.

"Yes."

He turned.

"Mr. Baker, this is Nathan Warner and I'm Ann Taylor. You wrote and asked—"

"Yes," he said with just a slight grimace of impatience. "I'll be happy to talk with you, but right now it's time for the auction to begin and I must see to it. I'll be with you just as soon as possible."

"But," Ann stuttered as he continued on with the vase.

"Please," he said firmly. "One of my assistants will relieve me after we get going. I won't be too long, I promise you."

A small sigh of disgust escaped from Ann as she watched him retreat.

"Now don't get your dander up," said Nathan. "We'll get this straightened out."

He took her arm and led her to a chair. "Here," he said, as he handed her the bidding card, "hold this. I'm going to get us some wine."

"Hide that thing," said Ann in exasperation. "I have a feeling that flicking it the wrong way could be disastrous."

"You really are a fussbudget when you want to be, aren't you?" he laughed.

"Well, maybe so, but I'm not pleased with the way this is going so far."

"Relax," he said as he headed for the wine. "I don't think that vase is worth all that much."

She gave him an annoyed look as he headed for the bar. When he returned Mr. Baker was calling for order and began with practiced, polished ease to joke and jolly the

167

crowd into a buying mood. Almost as if to mock Ann's bidding paranoia he brought out a beautiful crystal bell and started the bidding at only a few dollars, ultimately letting it go for ten.

Ann sat, feeling somewhat chagrined, as she met Nathan's amused grin. In the next few minutes a decanter went for thirty dollars and then a painting for five hundred dollars. As the cards flashed and the money toted up she gave Nathan a smug look and noted him pushing the bidding card deeper into his pocket.

"And now, ladies and gentlemen," she heard Mr. Baker saying about forty-five minutes later.

They had just auctioned a diamond and emerald necklace and earrings for nearly fifty thousand dollars and Ann could sense Nathan's growing shock.

"We have something very rare and special," Baker went on as he reached for the vase.

Ann noted an immediate snap to attention from four or five areas of the room. For the first time, she noted the security guard who had been hovering close to the vase throughout the afternoon.

"From the Warner estate in Philadelphia," Ann heard him saying.

An audible gasp escaped from her.

"This is a genuine fourteenth-century Chinese bottle. The pear shape and artistic decoration is especially significant. It's a museum item, ladies and gentlemen, and we'll begin the bidding at one hundred thousand dollars."

Ann thought Nathan was going to fall from his chair.

"For Pete's sake, Nathan, we have to do something!" she hissed. "That bottle is your vase! I'd stake my life on it. It's obvious how the mistake was made."

168

In less than thirty seconds the price was up to two hundred thousand dollars.

"All right," said Nathan, "we'll see to it, but right now let's just ride this out. You have the proof, don't you?"

"Sure," she said, "but—"

"Well, let's just wait and see what it gets!"

Ann was incredulous. It was almost as if Nathan thought he was in a grain market or something. As they sat in almost stupefied shock ninety seconds later the price went up to six hundred eighty thousand dollars. There had been heated bidding from several areas, but now the word "sold" rang out as a gentleman from the Metropolitan Museum of Art won out.

"Nathan, for heaven's sake get over there to Baker and insist that we talk to him now!"

Ann was so agitated that Nathan's calm was almost like a miracle to her. Slowly he rose and walked resolutely toward the auctioneer who was now at the sidelines speaking with the successful bidder. Nathan walked with an assured grace and purpose, the natural attribute of an honest, determined man.

"Mr. Baker," he said. "I beg your pardon, but I believe we'd better talk about that bottle you just sold. I think an honest mistake has been made."

"Please," said Mr. Baker, as he looked meaningfully toward the buyer. "I think we can discuss this a little later . . ."

"I think not," said Nathan firmly, as he gestured to Ann for the slides and other papers. "We've been trying to discuss this ever since we arrived more than two hours ago. I think we need to get the original ownership straightened out."

"Just what are you talking about?" asked an arrogant voice at his elbow.

Ann and Nathan turned to meet the glaring eyes of a haughty woman who had come to Mr. Baker's side.

"Mildred," said Baker, "do you know anything about this?"

"Vaguely," she said. "I do recall a call or two and we sent a letter about a vase, but surely that can't have anything to do with this bottle!"

Baker had managed to move them all away from the auction area to another smaller anteroom which he was using as an office.

"There can be no question about this," the woman fumed. "The Warner estate was one of our most valuable, filled with museum pieces."

"Yes, it does all seem very odd," said Mr. Baker, as he looked over Ann and Nathan suspiciously as if to give them a chance to back off.

"Now just a minute! What are you trying to say?" Nathan demanded as Ann saw a flush begin to rise over his collar. "I have a letter asking me to come here and identify my property and I'm saying that's my property." He gestured towards the vase. "We have proof of ownership," he said, handing the shipping receipt and slides over to Baker. "Examine these and I'm sure this will be cleared up immediately."

Mildred sniffed in derision as Baker turned to her.

"Well, doesn't it seem strange that they refer to their article as a vase, when clearly this is a bottle?"

"Not at all," said Ann as she finally got her wits about her enough to speak. "This was a keepsake of Nathan's ancestors who were missionaries in China during the last century. We found it along with lots of other things in a trunk. We assumed it was a vase because it had dried petals in it and we suspected that it might be valuable."

"Well, I just don't see how this could be," insisted Mildred.

"Well, we'd better check this out," said Baker, as he held the slides up to the light. "Of course, these days you hear of all types of sophisticated scams—you know, just about anyone could take a slide. . . . You aren't by any chance a relative of these other Warners, are you?"

"Now that's the last straw," said Nathan. "Those slides are duplicates of that bottle. We have shipping receipts and we've called you people repeatedly. Now I think you'd better start to show some consideration to my claim before I start to make some accusations of my own."

Ann knew Nathan was really angry and despaired now of any sort of amicable understanding. Throughout the discussion the buyer had remained, listening attentively, while he continued to examine the bottle.

"Did you say something about petals?" the buyer interrupted. "You know, there seems to be something inside." He maneuvered two fingers into the opening and retrieved a small yellowed envelope. "Look what I've found."

"Oh, yes," said Baker. "Yes. Perhaps this will solve the problem. Mildred, get the manifest and see exactly what was catalogued in for the Warner estate."

He reached for the envelope as the woman began to shift through some papers.

"I do recall this now," he went on. "When we appraised the bottle we found this in the bottom—practically the same color as the vase, covered with dust. Now what did you say your ancestors' names were?"

There was a calculating gleam in his eye.

Nathan looked at him in confusion.

"Why, John, John and Melissa," cried Ann.

Baker glanced through the letter and looked aghast. "Mildred," he said menacingly.

"Yes, it's John and Melissa," repeated Ann excitedly, reaching for the letter. "I feel like I almost know them . . . I've read so many of their letters. They had such a beautiful relationship . . ." Her voice trailed off as she silently read the stilted, yet poignant, loving lines of the letter.

Dearest John,

You made a terrible mistake and I've found it hard to forgive you. Now you're sad and unhappy and I'm sorry because I truly miss the happy man that I married. Too late I realize, in spite of your transgression, how much I love you, how very important you are to me and how very sad and desolate I am now that I seem to have lost you.

Please bring your spirit back to me whenever you can, but until you can, remember that I love you. Somehow losing you hurts more than anything you might have done. I know that now. Forgive me for not forgiving you.

All my love,
Melissa

P.S. I picked these flowers in memory of our first walk together.

She looked up and met Nathan's eyes as she brushed tears from her own. She felt a piercing pain and suddenly knew this letter was much more than just a means of identifying the owner of the vase.

"Mildred, let's get this straightened out," said Baker in the background. He was clearly annoyed. "We don't have room for sloppy work in our firm. We're trusted and our reputation . . ."

"Oh, Mr. Baker," broke in Mildred, totally contrite now. "I've found it. It's just an incredible coincidence and one of our clerks made a terrible error. All of the original documents are here from Miss Taylor, but she said she was representing Mr. Warner. It arrived on the very same day as this estate and . . ."

"Well, Mr. Warner," said Baker, now completely chagrined. "It seems you were right. A clerical error has been made and I apologize. I'm sure you can understand that we must be careful."

Nathan nodded and pulled Ann a little closer. Ann was gazing about numbly as she continued to clutch the letter. The love between the couple she had thought was so perfect was not after all. This should have been a happy moment, but somehow she felt betrayed.

"But now," she heard Baker through a haze, "we *have* just sold this magnificent bottle." He gestured toward the buyer. "Am I to assume, Mr. Warner, that that was your intent in sending it to us?"

"Well, I think initially we wanted it appraised so we could sell it, didn't we, Ann?"

"Nathan, it's your property," she cried.

"No," he said firmly. "We're in this together."

His eyes met hers in a deep communication. Suddenly the letter seemed to grow warm in her hands. For the first time she began to feel like it was all right to love him again.

"I really want that bottle," said the buyer.

"You've got it," said Nathan, as he reached for Ann's hand and gave it a little squeeze.

Ann responded with a mournful grimace. She was confused, not sure of her feelings.

"May I keep this letter?" she asked softly.

"Of course," Nathan said as he gave her a puzzled look.

The next hour was a flurry of activity as the details about the bottle were completed. Finally they had dinner in a quiet restaurant and began the long drive home. They had chattered and laughed incessantly about the events of the afternoon. It was as if all their adversities had been wiped away, yet Ann continued to feel subconscious pricklings of unease. She felt as if something were clutching at her, getting ready to pull her into a thousand pieces, but Nathan was so overjoyed and totally incredulous that his happiness won out and carried her along in a quasi-camaraderie.

"You know," he said, "you have to share this with us. Your knowing those names was something else. What does that letter say, anyway?"

She hesitated.

For a second she almost decided to pull it out and read it to him, but something stubborn kept her from doing it. She felt her pride lock her resolve. She needed time to think this through.

"Oh, it's just a note," she said. "Someone sending someone flowers."

When they finally reached home late that night Ann's earlier coolness had slowly returned. As the miles had ticked away she once again put everything into perspective as her thoughts turned darkly inward. She knew whatever the transgression between John and Melissa it could not rival the complete breach of trust displayed by Nathan.

The silence had grown longer and longer until finally the warmth of earlier moments became a poignant echo, and Nathan drove on, glancing at her now and then with a growing sense of uneasiness.

"Well," she said in dismissal when she got out of the car, "I'm happy for you."

"For both of us," he said as he sprang around to walk her to the door.

"No, don't get out," she said too late. "And forget about me. I didn't expect anything from this. I'm sure those pompous idiots would have gotten it straightened out eventually."

The air was brisk and cold as Nathan hustled her toward the door.

"Good night," she said, as she stopped and turned resolutely at the door. "You know, there's one good thing about all of this. Now you can buy the Harding farm and never have to worry about me or a conglomerate again."

Inwardly she gasped in shock. She didn't know where those words had come from. Nathan looked at her strangely. She saw something in his eyes flicker.

"Okay," he said. "Okay . . ." The mask was coming down. "I get the message," he continued through tight lips. "I can see that you won't let it go. You enjoy seeing me grovel too much."

His eyes were cold and hard. "Don't worry," he said. "I won't *ever* bother you again."

Ann looked at him completely bewildered. Before she could speak he was gone. She looked after him, an expression of sadness on her face. Then, with a heavy sigh, she fumbled for her keys and whispered, "Good-bye, Nathan."

CHAPTER TWELVE

She went through the door feeling an almost unbearable, confused sadness. The phone began to ring as she removed her coat. She glanced at her watch in alarm. Her voice was anxious as she answered.

"Ann?"

"Yes," she answered, really puzzled now as Randolph's boisterous voice came through the receiver.

"I have the most marvelous news and I just couldn't wait to call you. You'll have to blame Australia's time for the outrageous hour."

"What on earth?"

"I'm going back to Australia," he went on enthusiastically. "I've just been awarded a million-dollar grant to develop underground houses back home!"

"Why, that's wonderful," said Ann and realized it really was. "But I had no idea that you were even thinking of such a thing."

"Well, actually, it's a fantastic dream which I never thought would come true, so I just kept it to myself."

"Well, I must say this is going down as a landmark day." She went on to describe the earlier events of her day and the fantastic sale of the vase, now officially a bottle.

"I'm astounded, just astounded," he said in genuine amazement. "But now, where does that leave you?"

"Right where I was before," she said. "Nothing has changed except obviously I'll soon be losing the company of a very good friend. You know, I'm really going to miss you . . . In so many ways you often reminded me of my brother, Jeff."

"I know," he said.

The inflection in his voice was obvious. She could almost see a little grimace on his face. For a second she felt a real pang of regret.

"I don't suppose," she heard his deep voice say with a hint of laughter, "you've ever considered living in Australia?"

"No, no," she laughed with a comradely understanding, "I can honestly say I *have* not."

"Just as I thought," he said. "Well then, might I assume that it's safe to tell you about a young lady who has?"

"Why, you stinker," she said, now genuinely amused. "What have you been keeping from me?"

"Would you believe that my fellow grantee is a beautiful young lady who just happens to be a gifted architect, too?"

"How exciting," said Ann. "It sounds like it's going to be a wonderful project."

They continued to speak for a few moments longer. When they finally said their good-byes, which were a combination of euphoria and sadness, the mood also seemed appropriate for her farewell from Nathan. She went wearily to hang up her coat and saw the corner of the letter protruding from the pocket where she had alternately clutched it and shoved it away from her all evening. She retrieved it and straightened it gently. She opened it and read it one more time. Then with a sigh she carried it to the Warner trunk she had brought with her when she moved and dropped it in, on top.

She slept fitfully and awoke with an undeniable sense of sadness. When she walked about her house the next morning she felt lonely for the first time since she'd moved in. She was sure she wouldn't hear from Nathan and now Randolph would soon be leaving, too. She was really lost. Her footsteps seemed to retrace themselves and ended ultimately, time and time again, in front of the trunk. The letter lay there like an accusing finger, but she refused to touch it or read it again. As the vision of Nathan's retreating back played over and over she was beginning to feel an incredible sense of guilt and with it a stubborn familiar resentment began to build. Twice she went to the phone, but she couldn't bring herself to call. Yet everything in her shrieked to do it. The word "fool" began to form and shape and spell itself over and over until at last she put her coat on in disgust and went to see her parents.

As the days went by they grew longer and lonelier. The joy of the approaching Christmas season seemed to mock her. She took long walks and came to know the winter creatures intimately as she followed tracks and filled her bird feeders faithfully. She knew she needed to do something about shopping and was just resolutely forcing herself to go out on the next snowy Saturday morning when she heard the unmistakable jingle and swishing of a horse and sleigh coming into her drive. She looked out and saw Tanya and Christopher coming up to the door.

Their youthful enthusiasm and boisterousness was infectious, and she greeted them with a wide smile as she flung the door open in welcome.

"Come in, come in," she said. "I'm so glad to see you! Where did you get that sleigh?"

"Been in the family for years," said Christopher.

His face lit up as Ann gave both of them a big hug.

"You wouldn't believe the check we just got," said Tanya with relish, as they both knocked the snow from their boots. "Dad's just sitting in the chair looking at it. Grandpa's in shock, too."

"Well, I'm so happy for all of you," said Ann. "Now what else are you up to for excitement?"

"Oh, nothing much," said Christopher a little evasively.

"Not much," hooted Tanya. "He has a recital competition coming up next week and he's going to die if you don't come."

"Is that true, Christopher?" Her face was a picture of delight.

"Yeah, I really was hoping you would come."

"I wouldn't miss it," she said, "but right now there's something I'm dying to do that I've never done before."

"What's that?" they chorused.

"Take a ride in a horse and sleigh," she said conspiratorially.

"Well, let's go," they shouted.

In seconds she was bundled into warm clothes and they were out and away, whizzing over the back roads and fields until finally they pulled into the Warner drive. Ann was so flushed and exhilarated as she laughed and fell in love with these kids all over again that she hadn't given a thought to the possibility of seeing Nathan. When Grandpa Warner emerged from the house to greet them she thought she saw just a bit of disappointment on the teen-agers' faces when he said Nathan had gone to the bank.

An hour later they were all back at her house, frozen and happy as the room filled with laughter and the aroma of toasting marshmallows over the fire. Finally, as they were leaving, Ann spied the trunk again.

"Listen, while you're at it, how about taking your trunk back with you?"

Christopher looked at her in confusion for just a second. His eyes locked with Tanya's.

"I don't think it would fit in the sleigh," said Tanya quickly. "We'll ask Dad to stop over."

"Or you could drop it off on your way to work or something. Here. I'll put it in your car before I go," said Christopher.

Ann was honestly aghast as she watched this obvious conspiracy, but she also felt a special warm affection and did nothing to stop Christopher as he hoisted the trunk and waited for her to lead the way.

"Okay," she said, laughing. "I guess that would be the best way to do it."

A few days later, on a particularly cold and dismal afternoon, she decided she'd carried the trunk around long enough. As she pulled slowly up the Warner drive she tried to rehearse what she was going to say and finally decided on something short and quick. But, before she could say anything, she saw Grandpa Warner coming from the barn. He waved and came over to open her door.

"Go on up to the house," he said. "I've got some calves to feed. Nathan's inside getting ready for income taxes. He could use something to cheer him up!"

Her heart sank. *Great,* she thought.

Deciding not to prolong this any longer than necessary, she was attempting to wrestle the trunk from her car, her derriere protruding in a rather awkward position. She felt a strong pair of hands around her waist lifting her from behind.

"Now what are you trying to do?"

There was amusement in his voice, but his eyes were cold as she turned to greet Nathan.

"Bringing back your trunk," she stammered, as she brushed back her hair, which blew merrily beneath a snug winter cap.

He looked at her with a touch of impatience and reached in and easily retrieved it from her car. He hoisted it to his shoulder and Ann was again immediately aware of his magnetism as she followed behind him silently.

When they stepped through the door and he deposited the trunk safely she looked away uneasily.

"I . . . I can only stay for a minute. I'm on my way back to the office."

She glanced around the room, wanting desperately to avoid his eyes. Something seemed different. Mona's picture was gone from the mantle. She sensed that he had noticed her discovery, but he said nothing.

"Well. I just thought, under the circumstances and everything . . ." She cursed herself as she groped for words. "I thought you'd probably like to have this trunk back. It really is an important family heirloom."

She twisted her hands and turned to leave. "Everything's there—all of the letters and everything. They . . . Your ancestors were really a wonderful couple."

She brushed back her hair nervously and could no longer avoid the snare of his eyes. She could feel her legs weakening and thought again of the poignant lines of the letter she had left in the top of the trunk.

"Guess I'd better get going," she said finally.

She was sure her confusion was going to overwhelm her as he continued to peruse her with a hypnotic stare.

"I appreciate your stopping by," he said. "You're right,

181

that old trunk will probably be pretty interesting from now on."

She was moving towards the door. "Tell Christopher I wish him luck tomorrow night. I know he'll be terrific."

"Sure thing," he said.

She met his eyes one last time and saw the strength and stubbornness in the set of his jaw. His eyes spoke eloquently and questioned, but somehow the frost of their past few meetings won out as both of them allied with their pride.

She was shivering with cold as she tried to start her car a few seconds later. It took a minute or two before she got it going. Finally as it spurted and coughed to life she jerked past the window of the room she had just left. A light was on and Nathan was standing before the open trunk reading a letter. She wondered fleetingly if it was the one that had tortured her heart for so many days. As the motor smoothed out and picked up momentum she felt tears coming and did nothing to check them. When she turned from the lane she looked back one last time and saw Nathan watching her retreat from the window. He still held the letter in his hand.

The next night as Ann pulled up to the auditorium she was surprised by the number of cars there. When she went inside it was hushed and dim, but she could see the chairs for several judges. The stage was decorated with poinsettias and pine boughs, which created a pleasant aromatic background. The curtain was open and Ann could see that in addition to his own instruments Christopher was going to be accompanied by a bass fiddle, an oboe, and also by a tympani.

She was honestly impressed. She was sure Christopher

would do well, but she had no idea that he would attempt anything so complex.

"Can you believe this?" an excited voice asked at her elbow.

Ann turned and responded to the smiling Dale Spencer with a happy handshake.

"Nathan," the teacher went on, "sprang for all of this! Christopher hasn't spent a penny of his own money."

The auditorium was filling up and Ann saw Nathan, Tanya, and Grandpa Warner coming in. As they headed for the front she went toward the opposite corner while she busied herself conversationally with Dale Spencer. As he left her she fingered the program and finally acknowledged Nathan's eyes as he looked across the room toward her. Tanya saw her, too, and motioned for her to join them, but the seats were filling rapidly around them and the judges walked in, indicating that the recital was about to begin.

Dale left her hurriedly and Christopher and his accompanists came out and performed a light tune-up. Christopher seemed to be assured and confident, but Ann saw him look out to the audience. Nathan responded to him and then she gave him her own bright smile as the young man's eyes met hers.

She glanced through the program and was newly impressed. After some preliminary requirements of the competition, Christopher's original compositions and other arrangements carried the theme of the seasons and the rural world which surrounded him. As the lights dimmed and he stepped toward the front of the stage there was a bit of opening confusion as the stereotyped exercises were dispatched and then an incredible magic seemed to pervade the room. When the mournful and lively sounds of

183

the instruments blended their tones, the intricacies of the soil and seeds and seasons came to life in a weaving, caressing way almost to the point of creating an out-of-body experience.

The tympani came in with the roar of an approaching storm and suddenly Ann was transported across the room. She felt her spirit reaching out to Nathan. She sat transfixed, almost spellbound, as she relived again those first sensuous moments with him in the barn last spring. She remembered the smell of the hay and the strength of his hands. She knew she had loved him from that day on. As the music continued to cast its spell the rest of the year came plunging back. The walks, the talks, the day in the grove—it was all there, perfect and beautiful except for the fears they both admitted to . . . and except . . .

She could feel tears coming and she bit her trembling lips. She looked across the room and met Nathan's eyes floating in pools as deep as her own. The tempo of the music picked up and their laughter on the day they had visited the Amish, their wonderful hours of lovemaking, and Nathan's hesitant proposal came back again. Then pain racked her body. She thought bitterly of their terrible misunderstanding and suddenly the words in Melissa's letter took on a new clarity. As last she understood what it meant truly to forgive the unforgivable—something that only happened when love was more important.

As the concert continued, Ann yearned to reach out and touch Nathan, but now she was afraid it was too late. He had come to her, begged her to forgive him and she had shunned him. Even in a moment of great, ecstatic joy, just days ago, her heart had hardened towards him. She turned again, hoping to meet his eyes once more, but he was mesmerized by his son and the miracle occurring before him. Suddenly it was apparent to Ann that Nathan had at last realized that no matter what Christopher might become, his heritage was part of his soul and he would carry it wherever he went—whether by doing it as a farmer or passing on the message as a musician and composer, he would meet his responsibilities to the land and the farm.

As the concert ended with the mournful love song she had heard so long ago in the Warner living room, Ann heaved a great sigh and knew she had just participated in a wonderful experience. The room was electric with emotion as the judges addressed Christopher and Dale excitedly. Nathan and the others joined them and Ann went up hesitantly to voice her pleasure and congratulations.

"Wonderful" was echoed over and over.

As Ann gave Christopher a hug and turned to greet Tanya and Grandpa Warner she shyly acknowledged Nathan, too. When her hand touched his she knew she was lost forever and suddenly the grief and longing of the past few months was totally unbearable.

"I was very touched tonight," she said as she met his eyes again. "You must be very proud."

His granite features softened as his hand lingered, holding her own a warm, willing prisoner.

"Yes," he said. "Thanks to you I think I understand both of my kids a lot better now."

She smiled.

Suddenly it was as if they were entirely alone. The milling and hubbub swirled around them unnoticed. Ann realized, miracle of miracles, that another of those special moments had been granted. She looked in straight to Nathan's yearning heart and greeted the man she loved and she knew the rest was up to her.

"You know, Nathan, I wish I could write a letter as well as Melissa, but I think I finally understand what she was saying when she sent those flowers a hundred years ago."

He gave her a startled look for just a second and then complete understanding washed down over him. He began to step toward her just as Christopher came rushing to his side.

"Dad, Dad," he called excitedly. "I've scored a perfect score."

Ann smiled and Nathan did, too. Their eyes met again. "We'll talk," he promised.

An hour later as she drove home in pensive silence she felt a wonderful, incredible peace, yet she was troubled, too. She felt she must see and be with Nathan now, this very moment, before the magic could be lost again. Yet, she wouldn't steal anything from Christopher, either.

She arrived home and walked around in a special agony. She changed to something comfortable. She turned on soft music and sat before the fire sipping a sherry. An hour went by and the clock struck midnight, yet she couldn't sleep. She could feel the nearness of Nathan. She gave a start as she heard tires crunching through the snow. She went to the window and incredible joy filled her.

She rushed to open the door. Nathan was there and their glances met in an eloquent communication. They fell wordlessly into each other's arms. It was as though they had to have this one perfect communion of body and soul before anything could be spoken that might in any way interfere. All of the emotions, buried for so long beneath cloaks of unspoken grief, broke through their unnatural constraints and demanded that they be allowed to live again.

Slowly Nathan pulled her to him as he pushed the door

closed. He kissed her deeply and carried her through the door to the bedroom. His lips devoured her face hungrily as he smothered her with warm, urgent kisses. Slowly their bodies eased to the floor in the flickering shadows of the firelight from the cone-shaped hearth in the corner of the room. In utter, intense silence they devoured one another, unable to satisfy their raging passions until finally Nathan released her and began to carefully remove her robe. Their eyes locked together in mutual understanding and need. Carefully he unhooked her bra and gasped in admiration as her taut, fine breasts sprang free and beckoned his strong hands and lips to fondle them softly and sweetly. He continued his exercise in erotic wonderment as piece after piece of clothing came away from Ann's unresisting body until at last she lay before him in magnificent yearning.

Never once stopping the magic of his marauding fingers, she slowly unveiled his lean body until at last his urgency and state of undress matched her own. Slowly and wonderfully they came together in incredible tenderness until at last the pent-up, frustrated desires cascaded over them, demanded expression, and drew them into a frenzy of wild orgiastic delight. They clung to each other, breathless and spent and then, only then, did they dare to speak.

Leisurely Nathan began to massage the entire length of Ann's body in a calming, cherishing motion. She turned, contented and happy, toward him.

"I'm so glad you came here," she said softly. "I knew you would eventually, but I needed you tonight."

Nathan looked at her, bemused and serene. "I know," he said. "I felt the same way."

They gazed at each other in rapt wonderment as they shared a mutual soft kiss of endearment.

"Nathan," she said softly. "Could you come here and live in this house? Could you be happy here?"

"Sure," he said. "Why not?"

"Well," she hesitated. "It's just that you have such strong feelings about the family homestead . . ."

"Oh, hell, I think it's time that I moved on. Dad's still there in the house and there isn't any question that Tanya's going to take over the place. Knowing her she'll probably make the man she marries change his name to Warner!"

They both laughed.

"It doesn't bother you then that Randolph helped design and build this house?"

He looked at her quizzically. "Why should it? He's your friend. You had something special with him—probably still do, but I know what it is, just like you know about my past and where that stands now."

He took her by the shoulders and searched her eyes.

"This is here, now, today," he said firmly. "Believe me, I've got it all together and it adds up to one thing. You and me. Us. Here, together and the future starting from this day on. I can't think of a better place than this house where we can make our own history."

"Oh, Nathan," she smiled, as tears moistened her eyes. "I love you so much."

"I know," he said, as he began caressing her all over again, "but not nearly as much as I love you."

"Do you think," he laughed, "we can get a marriage license before Christmas? I'm all for going and getting a preacher out of bed right now."

"It can wait," she said as she responded to his touch, "at least until morning. . . ."

His lips began leaving a track of fire and suddenly she

felt like shouting her joy above the rooftops. Never again would she need to speak softly, except when her soul was in heaven and she knew that was where she was now.

"Speak softly," she whispered. "Speak softly to my soul, Nathan, the way you have from the very beginning."

LOOK FOR NEXT MONTH'S
CANDLELIGHT ECSTASY ROMANCES™